Beverley Nichols

The Wickedest Witch in the World

KNIGHT BOOKS
Hodder & Stoughton

ISBN 0 340 19785 4

Copyright © 1971 Beverley Nichols

First published in 1971 by W. H. Allen and Co Ltd

This edition first published 1977 by Knight, the paperback
division of Hodder & Stoughton Children's Books

Printed and bound in Knight Books for Hodder & Stoughton
Children's Books, a division of Hodder & Stoughton Ltd,
Arlen House, Salisbury Road, Leicester by Cox & Wyman Ltd,
London, Reading and Fakenham

For Lucia with love

Chapter One

*Once upon a time there was a little horse who was very ill-*treated by his mistress, who was a witch.

The name of the little white horse was Snowdrop and the name of the witch was Miss Smith.

Although Miss Smith looked very young, when she was wearing her wig and her false teeth and her false eyelashes and her lipstick—which was made out of snake's blood mixed into a smooth paste with the eyeballs of bats—she was in fact almost four hundred years old, having been born in the reign of Queen Elizabeth the First.

This is a great age, even for a witch, and when Miss Smith was nearing her four hundredth birthday she decided that the time had come for her to take things more easily. Although she was still very wicked, with a large experience of magic spells and deadly poisons, she found that after weaving any specially powerful spell she felt quite tired out. And sometimes she mixed up the labels on the poisons because her eyes were not so keen as they used to be.

For example there was one dreadful occasion, when she had been hired by a very wicked lady to throw a baby into convulsions. This was just the sort of job which Miss Smith enjoyed; she did not like babies, and she was only too anxious to throw them into convulsions. But unfortunately she mixed up the bottles, and instead of giving the baby her special Brimstone Convulsion Mixture she gave it an ordinary soothing syrup, so that the baby slept on peacefully and came to no harm at all. Which was of course very annoying for the lady who had hired her, and even more annoying for Miss Smith, who had to give the money back.

Shortly after this affair of the baby Miss Smith decided that she must definitely look out for a less exhausting occupation.

But what should she do? That was the question.

As she sat pondering this problem in her Mayfair flat (all the best modern witches live in Mayfair) she picked up a copy of *The Times*, which she read every morning in order to study the announcements of Births, Marriages, and Deaths. This was her favourite reading. If a baby had been born, and if she had nothing better to do, she would often decide to throw it into convulsions, just to pass a pleasant afternoon. If a young couple had got married she might divert herself by bringing the bride out in spots during the honeymoon. And if somebody had died, there was always the happy chance that it might be a person whom she had done away with herself.

But this morning, instead of turning to her usual column, she opened the page at the advertisements of 'Businesses for Sale'. And immediately one of the advertisements caught her eye. She read:

Small Laundry for Sale in Country Town
The laundry has only just been fitted with two beautiful
  new washing machines
Easily run by one person

As soon as Miss Smith read this advertisement her eyes gleamed, and several puffs of green smoke floated out of her nostrils. This was a sure sign that she was excited, and she was quite unable to control it. This weakness could sometimes be very awkward for her. For instance, if she suddenly got excited in a railway compartment, the green smoke would pour out of her nostrils, and she could not hide it even if she put a handkerchief over her nose. The other passengers thought this behaviour very strange, and once she was fined two guineas for smoking in a non-smoking carriage. Miss Smith felt that this was very unjust for she had not been smoking at all . . . merely letting off steam. However, she got her own back on the judge who had fined her, by covering him with warts.

But at this moment there was nobody watching her, so she let the green smoke pour out as much as it wanted. It was a most refreshing sensation.

A laundry! It was the very thing! The more she thought of the idea, the more it appealed to her. If there really were those two beautiful new washing machines they would do all the hard work, leaving her free to get up to all sorts of splendid tricks. Her mind leapt ahead, picturing the wonderful opportunities she would have for practising her skill. She would invent itching powders to put into the water in which she washed the sheets, so that any little boy who slept between them would feel as though he had been bitten by a thousand fleas. And special smelly powders for little girls' dresses, so that when they put them on and went to a party, all the other little girls would sniff and ask if they had stepped in something. There was no end to the nice, beautiful, beastly things she could get up to, and Miss Smith felt that this was indeed her lucky day.

And then, her eyes caught another advertisement, a little lower down.

Little White Horse for Sale
Answers to the Name of 'Snowdrop'
Very gentle and fond of children

Reasonable price in exchange for home where he will be
   well looked after.
Apply to the Vicarage, Meadowstream.

Once again Miss Smith's eyes gleamed, and once again the green smoke began to pour from her nostrils. A little white horse! If she was going into the laundry business what could be more ideal than a little white horse? She would be able to drive around when she was delivering the washing, and he would be a most wonderful advertisement. People would say 'Oh! What a beautiful little white horse Miss Smith has got! And what a wonderful washer-woman she must be! She must have some marvellous secret powder to wash him in, to get him so gleaming white! And we must certainly take all our washing to her so that we may be just as white as that little white horse.'

You may perhaps suspect that Miss Smith had a television set, and listened to the soap advertisements. They always enraged her, for Miss Smith did not like whiteness; she liked blackness. Often, when a deep voice boomed at her that Blank-O 'washes brightest of all', she would tremble with rage and so much green smoke would pour from her nostrils that she had to get up and adjust her set. Blackness was what *she* wanted. Even at this moment her wicked brain began to busy itself inventing a new soap which she would call Witch-O. This soap would wash everything beautifully white at first, but a few hours after people had put the things on, they would turn jet black . . . the things, of course, not the people. Witch-O would come in specially handy if she were ever called upon to wash a wedding dress. It would give the bridegroom quite a shock when he was putting the ring on his bride's finger, to see that she was suddenly clothed in black from head to foot, as though she were going to a funeral.

Then she had an even better idea. Instead of going to all the trouble of inventing the soap, she would see if Beelzebub could do it.

Now we must tell you about Beelzebub, and when you have heard his story, you will agree that he was a living proof of the fact that Miss Smith was quite the wickedest witch who ever walked this world.

Beelzebub was originally a lady-bird, and Miss Smith first met him in a graveyard, where she had gone to rest on a damp tombstone, which she always found more comfortable than an armchair. In those days Beelzebub was very young, hardly more than a baby; he was just a tiny red spot whom you would scarcely have noticed if you had seen him sitting on a leaf nibbling the insects that he liked for dinner. He was quite a good little thing at heart, but he had one serious fault. He was always playing truant, straying from home and causing a great deal of trouble before he was found again. One day he flew so far that he was completely lost, and when he could fly no farther he fluttered into the graveyard and sank exhausted on to the very same tombstone where Miss Smith was sitting.

The Witch's first instinct was to squash him, because she was very fond of squashing things. She put out her thumb to do so, and then she paused. He was obviously very young and very innocent, and she wondered if perhaps she could adopt him, teach him her evil tricks and train him in the way in which he should go—which, needless to say, was the way in which he should *not* go. So instead of squashing him, she lifted him up, put him carefully in her wig and carried him home.

That was how it all began. She took great pains in training him, teaching him how to bite and how to sting and mixing his food with deadly poisons so that they gradually got into his blood-stream, with the result that when he spat at people they came out in boils. She worked on his brain as well as on his body and when she had finished with him you would not have known that he had ever been a lady-bird at all; he looked more like a great big horrible beetle. Nor would you have known that he had ever had an innocent heart, for he seemed to be evil through and through.

Yes, Miss Smith was very pleased with the way in which she had educated Beelzebub and there was only one way in which he had disappointed her. She had wanted to make him black all over, but the nearest she got to changing the colour of his wings was to turn them dark purple.

'Never mind', she said to herself, 'the colour of his body isn't all that important. What really matters is the colour of his heart, which is black all through'.

Maybe she was right, and maybe she was not quite so right. We shall see. Meanwhile, Beelzebub's behaviour was certainly as wicked as she could ever have hoped.

But we were talking about her plans for the laundry.

'Beelzebub darling!' she cried, leaning back in her chair, and putting down the newspaper. 'Pockle-poop!'

By the way we forgot to mention that Miss Smith, in order to be quite sure that she had Beelzebub completely in her power, had gone to all the trouble of learning Beetle Language. This is one of the most difficult languages in the world. We shall not be using much of it in our story, but you might as well know that 'Pockle-poop' means 'Come here!'

'Spotty spittle?' rejoined the beetle, buzzing down from the mantelpiece. The translation of this is 'Do you want me to spit on something?' Which will be enough Beetle Language for the moment.

'Yes,' said Miss Smith. 'I do indeed want you to spotty-spittle on something. And I will show you what it is!'

She went over to the linen cupboard and took out a white handkerchief. 'That is what I want you to spotty-spittle on, my sweetheart. I want you to turn it black. Quite, quite black!'

Beelzebub could hardly believe his ears. He was always wanting to spotty-spittle on things but the witch very seldom let him do so, on account of the laundry bills. It seemed almost too good to be true that he was going to be allowed to spotty-spittle on such a fine white handkerchief.

'Yes, my sweet', Miss Smith assured him. 'You have my full permission. And remember, I want you to turn it black, black, *black*!'

Beelzebub crouched down, stared at the handkerchief to get his aim, and then—after taking a deep breath—he spotty-spittled. It landed right in the centre of the target and immediately the handkerchief began to change colour. First it went grey and then it went dark brown and finally it went black altogether.

'Splendid!' exclaimed the witch. 'I couldn't have done it better myself.'

Beelzebub jumped up and down with pleasure, fluttering his purple wings. 'More spotty-spittle?' he enquired eagerly.

'Not for the moment, darling. One treat is enough for today. But very soon you will have as much spotty-spittle as you could possibly want. We are going on a journey.'

Having made this promise, she went into the bathroom to change her wig, then she stuck on a fresh pair of false eyelashes and dabbed herself with rose-water. This always made her feel faintly sick, because she hated sweet perfumes and would have greatly preferred to smell something sour. However, she reflected, she was going into the world of humans, and when one mixes with humans, one must fall in with their horrid ways.

She went back to the sitting-room and picked up Beelzebub, placing him carefully on her wig so that he was comfortable among the golden curls. Then, with a final glance at herself in the looking-glass, she sallied forth, locking the door behind her. In the street she hailed a taxi to Waterloo Station where she bought a ticket for Meadowstream. Three hours later she was driving up the broad street of a quiet old country town, and knocking on the door of The Snowhite Laundry Limited.

Chapter Two

The lady who owned the laundry was called Miss Watkins, and the reason she was selling it was because her uncle had died and left her an ostrich farm in South Africa.

She was so excited by this that she could think of nothing else and as soon as she saw Miss Smith standing on the doorstep her first question was, 'Do you know anything about ostriches?'

Miss Smith thought this was rather a peculiar question in the circumstances, but she wanted to create a good impression, so she said, 'Yes, indeed I do.'

Miss Watkins breathed a sigh of relief. 'Thank heavens you have come,' she said. 'Tell me!'

'They bury their heads in the sand.'

Miss Watkins looked disappointed. 'I knew that already,' she said. 'Everybody tells me that they bury their heads in the sand. But surely they must have *some* other occupation?'

Miss Smith shook her head sadly. 'I am afraid not,' she replied. 'They are very set in their ways. And naturally, with their heads in this position, it makes conversation very difficult.' She was beginning to think that Miss Watkins must be slightly dotty. However, this might be to her own advantage. If Miss Watkins was as dotty as she seemed to be, she might be persuaded to sell the laundry for much less than it was worth. But first she must find out why she was so interested in ostriches.

'Well, it's like this,' said Miss Watkins. 'My uncle has

left me this ostrich farm in South Africa and I am going out there to manage it.'

A gleam of greed came into Miss Smith's eye. 'Is it a large farm?' she enquired.

'Enormous. With thousands of ostriches worth at least a million pounds.'

This was almost more than Miss Smith could bear. Why should a silly old woman like Miss Watkins get all this money for nothing, while *she* had to work so hard? Nobody had ever given *her* an ostrich. For a moment she felt like casting a spell over Miss Watkins—something very painful indeed. Then she thought better of it. Her wicked mind began to work overtime.

'I am so happy for you, Miss Watkins,' she gushed. 'All those beautiful birds and all those lovely feathers! You will make a fortune. There's only one thing you should guard against, though I'm sure you know all about it already.'

'And what would that be?'

'Ostrichitis!' Miss Smith pronounced the word with such a sinister hiss that Miss Watkins looked quite alarmed.

'Heavens!' exclaimed Miss Watkins. 'Whatever is ostrichitis?'

Miss Smith shook her head sadly. 'It is the most terrible disease,' she said. 'If your beautiful birds were to catch it, all their feathers would drop out, and then you would not make any money at all. But it would be even worse than that. Most of them would feel so ill that they would never be able to take their heads out of the sand again.'

'And then what would happen?'

'They would suffocate.'

Poor Miss Watkins was almost in tears. 'Oh, Miss Smith,' she cried, 'whatever shall I do?'

Miss Smith gave a tinkling laugh, 'Cheer up, my dear! By

an extraordinary chance, I happen to have a bottle of anti-ostrichitis in my bag at this very moment.'

Miss Watkins stared at her in bewilderment.

'What is anti-ostrichitis?'

'It is my own invention.' She drew out of her bag a small bottle filled with bright green liquid, which sparkled and bubbled in the sunlight. It looked as pretty as a jewel, but Miss Watkins would have shrunk back in horror if she had known what it was made of. The ingredients were sixteen squashed snails, the blood of one female octopus, three rancid vultures' eggs, seven ounces of frogs' spawn and one teaspoonful of bottled salad cream. This last item was the deadliest of them all.

Miss Smith was very proud of this recipe, as well she might be, for it had taken her a great deal of time and trouble.

'What a beautiful bottle!' Miss Watkins stretched out her hand towards it. As her fingers touched the glass, she gave a little scream. 'But it is as cold as ice,' she cried.

'Much colder,' retorted Miss Smith. 'One of these bottles is as cold as seventeen icebergs.'

'But what do I do with it?'

'As soon as you get to South Africa you mix it with water and you go up to the ostriches and pour it over their behinds.'

'And then what happens?'

'They take their heads out of the sand and their feathers start to grow.'

'How fast?'

'So fast that you can't keep pace with them.'

'How big do they grow?'

Miss Smith stretched her arms out at full length. 'As big as this!'

By now Miss Watkins was so excited that she would

have given almost anything for the bottle. But she was not quite dotty enough to believe everything that Miss Smith was telling her, unless she could be given some proof that it was really true.

Miss Smith knew exactly what she was thinking, because she could read peoples' minds like an open book. 'Very well,' she said to herself, 'I will give this silly old woman the proof she wants. I will work a spell.'

So she gave another of her tinkling laughs and looked around her. 'I suppose there are no ostriches in the house at the moment?'

Miss Watkins shook her head.

'Never mind. Any kind of bird will do. I see that there is a beautiful turkey walking about in your backyard. Might we pay him a visit?'

Before Miss Watkins could reply she had stepped into the backyard and was beginning to grind her teeth and make the hideous faces that she always put on when she was weaving spells. While doing this she kept her back turned to Miss Watkins, who would have been terrified if she could have seen her, because her nose grew long and sharp like a beak and her false teeth turned yellow and her mouth went bright green. All this was very exhausting for Miss Smith, and took a great deal out of her. But she only had to keep it up for a few seconds, for as soon as she had made herself hideous enough she was able to weave the spell, and she darted over to the turkey and sprinkled a drop of the green liquid on to its behind. Then she took out her handkerchief and pretended to blow her nose when, in fact, she was pressing it back into shape. At the same time, she rapidly slipped in a new pair of false teeth and smeared on some lipstick to cover up the green. So that when she turned round to face Miss Watkins, she was as pretty as ever.

And now the most extraordinary things began to happen to the turkey. The feathers of its tail began to tremble, as though they were being twitched by invisible fingers, and then they started to sprout and curl and went on sprouting and curling till they arched over its back. Most extraordinary of all, they came out in vivid shades of purple and orange and blue. Meanwhile, the poor creature was making loud noises of alarm and indignation. 'Gobble—gobble—gobble,' he cried. And again . . . 'Gobble—gobble—gobble—g-g-g-gobb-b-b-le.' He had every reason to be disturbed. Apart from the fact that his behind felt as though he had just sat in a bed of stinging nettles, there were the social problems to be considered. How could he explain all this to his friends? What would Mrs. Turkey think when she saw him? It was all extremely distressing, and his 'gobble—gobble—gobbles' became more and more frantic. Needless to say, Miss Smith had not the least sympathy for him. She merely regarded him with a cold smile, at the same time fingering her nose, which was still a little out of shape.

As for dotty old Miss Watkins . . . all *she* felt was that Miss Smith was the most wonderful young lady in the world, and that her bottle of green liquid was something which she must have at all costs. For if it could make turkeys grow ostrich feathers, what would it not do to real ostriches?

'Miss Smith,' she gasped, 'how much will I have to pay for your bottle of anti-ostrichitis?' 'Oh Miss Watkins, murmured the Witch, 'I would not dream of asking you to *pay* for it. Money means nothing to *me*, and I will gladly *give* it to you. All the same—as you have mentioned it, and as this has been such a happy meeting, perhaps you might care to give me something to remember you by?'

'Of course, of course,' agreed Miss Watkins eagerly 'Had you anything special in mind?'

'As a matter of fact, I had,' replied Miss Smith. 'I thought you might like to give me your little laundry.'

'My laundry?' This was not at all what Miss Watkins had expected. 'But how could I give you my laundry? It is up for *sale*.'

'I see.' Miss Smith's voice was not quite so friendly now. 'And you think that your little laundry is worth more than your ostrich farm?'

'That is not the point,' replied Miss Watkins crossly. She was beginning to feel quite hot and bothered. 'What I mean is . . .'

Miss Smith interrupted her. 'Well, madam,' she observed, 'you may be quite right. Your little laundry *may* be worth a great deal more than your ostrich farm. If all your ostriches develop ostrichitis, which is highly probable, and if all their tails fall off, your farm will be worth nothing at all. Not a penny.' She shook her head briskly. 'I know nothing about business, but I am quite certain that you will not be able to sell even *one* dead ostrich, let alone ten thousand dead ostriches. There is no sale for such creatures. None at all.'

Miss Watkins clasped her hands in despair. 'Oh Miss Smith, whatever shall I do?'

'Your remedy is very simple,' replied Miss Smith calmly. 'Give me your little laundry and I will give you this bottle of anti-ostrichitis. All you have to do is to sign on the dotted line.'

Even as she was speaking she drew from her handbag a document which had been prepared in advance by her lawyers.

'On the dotted line,' repeated Miss Smith.

And so powerful was the spell that she was casting over

her victim, that poor Miss Watkins signed without any further delay. For a worthless bottle of poisonous liquid she had made Miss Smith a present of one of the nicest little laundries in the country. And it had all happened in the space of twenty minutes.

If Miss Smith had not been such a very wicked person, we might almost be tempted to admire her for the speed and efficiency with which she worked during the course of the next hour. She helped Miss Watkins to pack her suitcase. She rang up the airport to book her a seat on the plane to South Africa. She even made her a cup of tea.

Anyway, within the hour, Miss Watkins had departed and Miss Smith was standing on the doorstep, waving her good-bye.

There was still work to be done.

Locking the door behind her, she stepped out and walked towards the vicarage, which lay at the other end of the street. She must get hold of that little white horse before anybody else was able to buy him.

As she was making her way, Betty—the vicar's nine-year-old daughter—was in the old stable talking to Snowdrop. As she talked, she nuzzled her dark curls against his snow-white mane, and a tear trickled down her cheek.

'Oh, Snowdrop,' she was saying, 'I don't know what I shall do when you have to leave us!'

By way of reply Snowdrop gave a gentle whinny. He was not sure what she was telling him but he had a feeling that it must be sad. And because he loved Betty very much, he felt sad too.

'If only there were some way to avoid it,' she went on. 'But Daddy says that there isn't. He says that there is hardly any money left to buy anything to eat, so what are we to do?'

Poor Snowdrop shook his head in bewilderment. He could think of no answer to such a question.

And then, suddenly, he pricked up his ears. In the distance he had heard the tinkle-tinkle of the front door bell. Usually it was a sweet and welcome sound; often it meant that Betty's friends had come to play and they would visit him after tea and talk to him and give him pieces of sugar. But today the bell sounded different . . . harsh and jangling and hostile, as though there were a crack in it. He felt like crying to his mistress: 'Don't answer that bell. Let it ring, please don't leave me. Whoever may be ringing that bell is a bad person who will only bring us both unhappiness.'

But even if he had been able to put these feelings into words he was too late. For already his mistress had run to answer it.

When she opened the door, Betty could hardly believe her eyes. Never had she seen such a beautiful young lady . . . such golden tresses, such fluttering eyelashes, such red lips and such gleaming teeth.

'Good afternoon,' said Miss Smith. 'Have I the honour of speaking to Miss Betty Gray?'

'Y . . . y . . . yes,' stammered Betty. Nobody had ever suggested that it was an honour to speak to her before.

'I believe you have a pony for sale?'

Betty's heart gave a jump. Although she dreaded the thought of parting from Snowdrop she could imagine no nicer person than Miss Smith for him to go to.

'Yes, we have,' she said. 'He is a very beautiful pony and his name is Snowdrop.'

'What a pretty name!' exclaimed Miss Smith. Which

only goes to show what a deceitful creature she was. For she did not think that Snowdrop was a pretty name for a pony at all. If he had been called Toadstool or Stinkpot she would have thought that those were *very* pretty names. Or if he had been called Hogwash or Greedyguts. But she detested the very idea of a Snowdrop. However, she disguised her feelings with a smile.

'Too pretty!' repeated Miss Smith. 'Might I see him?'

'Of course,' said Betty. 'Will you come with me?'

She led the way across the lawn towards Snowdrop's stable.

As soon as Snowdrop saw Miss Smith peering at him over the door of his stall he began to tremble all over, as though he had caught a sudden chill. He could not explain this sensation, because—to the outward eye—she looked so very charming. All he knew was that she made him feel cold and frightened and that he wished she would go away.

'Here he is,' said Betty.

'I think he is the nicest pony I ever saw,' remarked Miss Smith. 'And I will certainly buy him.'

As soon as he heard these words the pony trembled more than ever.

'Why, Snowdrop, whatever is the matter?' exclaimed Betty. 'You mustn't look so frightened. This young lady is going to give you a beautiful new home.' She turned to Miss Smith. 'That *is* true, isn't it?'

'Of course it is true,' said Miss Smith. 'A *very* beautiful new home.'

'There, you see! So you should be happy, Snowdrop darling, instead of looking so miserable.'

'Perhaps he is just shy,' suggested Miss Smith. 'So let us leave him for the moment and talk business.'

'I am afraid that my daddy is not very well,' said Betty,

as she led the way back to the house. 'So perhaps you would not mind talking business with me?'

'Not in the least. It is just a question of the price. How much would you like for dear Snowdrop?'

'I think that my daddy was hoping that we might get five pounds.'

Miss Smith raised her eyebrows. 'Five pounds? That seems a great deal of money.' In fact, as she well knew, it was not nearly enough for such a beautiful pony.

Betty hesitated. She knew that her father was very poor, and that Snowdrop *had* to be sold. So she said 'Well, perhaps he would not mind taking four pounds.'

Miss Smith sighed and then gave a charming smile. 'Very well.' She opened her bag and drew out four pound notes. As she pressed them into the little girl's hand Betty noticed that her fingers were icy cold, and she wondered why such a beautiful young lady should have such cold fingers on such a warm summer's day.

'So that's settled then,' continued the witch. 'And may I take him with me now?'

Betty was trying very hard not to cry. 'This very minute?'

'Yes, my dear.' She smiled again. 'You see, he belongs to me now. So will you please go and fetch him?'

Betty turned away. She could not trust herself to speak. Even when she reached Snowdrop, she could not say good-bye to him, not in so many words. She could only put her arms round his neck, and give him a final kiss. When she brought him back to Miss Smith she handed her the reins in silence and walked back to the garden, which suddenly seemed cold and empty. And she did not watch him go.

That was how Snowdrop came into the witch's clutches, and that was the beginning of all his troubles. They were not long in coming, for no sooner had she got him home, than she turned on him with a snarl and struck him a stinging blow across the nose. Then she tugged him to the old barn which was to be his stable, pushed him inside and slammed the door.

For a few moments she stood there, basking in the sunlight. From a corner of the yard, the turkey watched her, feeling very sad, and wondering why his world seemed suddenly to have turned upside down. His behind was still stinging, and he could not get used to these absurd ostrich feathers sticking out at the back.

'Gobble—gobble—gobble,' he cried. 'Gobble—gobble—gobble.'

Miss Smith threw him a vicious glance. 'Shut up,' she hissed.

'Gobble—gobble—gobble,' cried the turkey again. 'Gobbledy—gobbledy—g-g-obbledy.'

'I'll give you gobbledy—gobbledy,' snarled Miss Smith. And before the turkey knew what was happening, she had darted over and wrenched the longest of his feathers from his tail with a single tug. The poor creature felt as though he had had a tooth out and ran away in terror, scrambled over the wall and made for the open fields.

'Serve him right,' snapped Miss Smith. 'Nobody gobbles at me and gets away with it!'

Her face crinkled into a wicked smile. Everything was coming her way at last. 'And about time too,' she thought, 'after four hundred years. If one goes on being wicked long enough, one is bound to get one's reward.'

She gave a long sigh of satisfaction. Yes, everything was coming her way. Even the problem of her catering seemed to be settled. For out of the corner of her eye she had noticed a nice cluster of toadstools growing in the shadow of the yard. Several very juicy slugs were crawling over them. They would make a delicious soup for supper.

Chapter Three

So far in this story we seem to have been meeting a lot of very unpleasant people. Or at any rate one very unpleasant person, because you will probably agree that Miss Smith is quite the most unpleasant person you ever heard about.

Meanwhile, it is time that we met some nice people for a change.

In order to meet the first of them, we have to look up into the branches of a tree.

It is an enormous tree; in fact it is the most enormous tree in England. Very few people have ever seen it and—this is the interesting thing—it has never been seen by anybody over the age of twelve. If you are over twelve years old you cannot see this tree at all. You can only feel that it is there. A great many grown-up people know that the tree *is* there, and they may take you along to see it one day. They will put you in the car and drive you through the country lanes and then they will stop the car outside a little gate, look through a gap in the hedge and say to you . . . 'There is your tree.' They will say this rather sadly, because they know and you know too that they cannot really see it. They are too old. But you can see it. And you can get out of the car, push open the gate and run across the field through the long grasses and the buttercups and look up into the branches of the tree.

When you do you will be greatly surprised, because you will see an old lady sitting in it. Her name is Mrs. Judy and the reason she spends so much time sitting in the tree is simply because she likes doing so. If you were to ask her why she likes it she would shrug her shoulders and say, 'I don't know. I just like it.' Which seems a sensible sort of reply.

At the foot of the tree is a small house, which was built for her round the trunk by her grand-daughter Judy, a very pretty girl of twelve who always stays with her for the holidays. When Judy first began to build the house her grandmother was very annoyed. 'You are like all the rest of them,' she said. 'You are trying to get me to come down from my tree and I won't have it. You can stay in your house, but I won't set a foot inside it.'

'But, Granny,' replied Judy, 'You are growing very old and you can't stay in the tree for ever.' 'Oh yes, I can,' she insisted, with an indignant snort. 'And I shall.' But one day it began to rain, and it went on raining and raining, and Mrs. Judy was soaked to the skin and caught a terrible cold so that she had to come down. Once she had stepped inside the house she was obliged to admit that it was very comfortable and she agreed to sleep in it. But whenever the weather is sunny and warm she still spends a great deal of time in the tree, though nowadays she very seldom goes up into the higher branches. As Judy had reminded her, she is growing very old, though she refuses to admit it. She says that the reason she does not go up to the higher branches any longer is because the view is not so good from there as it is from the lower ones. Between you and me, this is not quite true, as the view is really much better from the top. However, she is such a nice old lady that we can forgive her these little vanities.

The time has now come to tell you about Mrs. Judy's Invention.

She had always been interested in magic and if she had

not been such a nice old thing she might have made a very powerful witch—even more powerful than Miss Smith. But she was not that sort of person; she liked to use her talents to make people happy. And not only people, but animals. In fact, if she had been given the choice of helping a lame dog over a stile or helping a lame millionaire into his motor-car, she would have chosen the dog every time.

Now the thing which had always worried Mrs. Judy about animals was the fact that they could not speak. If a kitten had lost its way it could not tell you its name or address; if a pony had a pain it could not tell you where the pain was; and if a dog was being starved or ill-treated it could not make a complaint to the right authorities. All these poor creatures had to suffer in silence. If only she could invent something which would help the animals to speak! Well, one day she did invent just this very thing. And at about the time when our story was beginning, she had nearly brought it to perfection.

She called it Mrs. Judy's Patent Animal Translator. It was shaped like an old-fashioned gramophone, with a huge wooden trumpet and a handle on the side to wind a clockwork motor. In front of the machine there was a pink satin cushion on which the animal sat when it was going to speak and as soon as it began the clockwork started to turn, setting off a sort of magic typewriter which 'translated' the sounds into words.

When Mrs. Judy first began, the machine was very crude and simple. For instance, if a kitten purred into the trumpet all the typewriter could do was to translate the purr into the single word 'happy'. Or if a puppy whined all it could do was to write the single word 'unhappy'. But gradually, as she experimented, she made the typewriter bigger and bigger, with many new words and letters, so that instead of just writing 'unhappy' it wrote, 'I am unhappy because I have been beaten.' As time went by, she added more and more words and letters and put in three more clockwork motors. Most important of all, she discovered that if she snipped off a little piece of an animals' fur, and rubbed it gently over the paper on which the machine was typing, the paper became so sensitive that the machine started typing six times as fast and put down the most extraordinary things that she could never have found out of her own accord. The first time this happened was with a stray sheepdog. When he sat down on the pink cushion some of his fur got caught in the machine, which was so painful for him that he began to howl. Whereupon the machine started off at top speed and only a few moments later it had written, 'I have been beaten by a man with a big black beard who lives on a farm by the side of a lake.' This was a wonderful moment in Mrs. Judy's life. Like all great inventors she needed a stroke of luck and here it was. By sheer chance the stray sheepdog had shown her that if her Translator was really to get results she must feed a little piece of fur into it.

Now we must return to Miss Smith.

After Miss Smith had cast her spell on the turkey, which made his behind come out in ostrich feathers, the poor creature was so bewildered that he had rushed away from her, helter-skelter, out into the open fields. He had no idea where he was going; all he knew was that he must escape from her at all costs. And it was only by chance that he followed a path leading through the woods to the valley where Mrs. Judy had her house under the tree.

When the turkey saw the smoke coming out of the chimney in the distance, he sat down by the side of a stream to collect his thoughts. His first instinct had been to run straight up to the house and ask for shelter, but how could he be sure that they would take him in? They might merely laugh at him, and think that he was putting on airs, wearing these ridiculous feathers. On the other hand, it was just possible that they might be people who would understand. They might even get a pair of scissors and cut them off. The thought of being rid of them, once and for all, and becoming an ordinary turkey again, made up his mind. So he struggled to his feet—and set out to see what lay in store.

When Judy saw the turkey coming towards her she could scarcely believe her eyes. Obviously, it *was* a turkey, and it was gobbling away at the top of its voice, but what were all those feathers doing on its behind?

'Granny, Granny!' she cried up into the tree. 'There is the strangest creature coming to see us!'

'What is strange about it?' enquired Mrs. Judy sleepily. She did not like being woken up from her afternoon nap.

'It has a lot of ostrich feathers coming out of it.'

'In which case,' retorted Mrs. Judy tartly, 'it is presumably an ostrich.'

'But it is *not* an ostrich,' insisted Judy. 'It is a turkey. Listen!'

'Gobble, gobble, gobble,' cried the turkey, coming nearer and nearer.

Mrs. Judy frowned, rubbed her eyes, and sat up. 'Never a moment's peace,' she thought to herself. 'Turkeys and ostriches, all mixed up together. What is the world coming to? What will they think up next?' All the same, she felt something strange was in the air— something that she did not like at all. So she climbed down from her branch, and went to find out what was happening.

As soon as she saw the turkey, her heart went out to it, as it did to all creatures in distress. The poor thing was trembling all over, and it kept on glancing over its shoulder at the feathers, and then looking up at her, as though it were ashamed of them. And its 'gobble—gobble's were growing fainter and fainter, as though it had said all it had to say, and could think of nothing more.

A gleam came into Mrs. Judy's eye. She rubbed her hands together in excitement.

'My Translator,' she cried. 'We must sit him in front of my Translator!'

Judy hesitated. She was very fond of her granny and she had a great respect for her magic powers. But she was a very modern little girl and—quite frankly—she did think that the Translator was rather old-fashioned.

'What are we waiting for?' demanded Mrs. Judy. 'Sit him in front of the Translator!'

'But, Granny,' protested Judy, 'what good will it do if he only goes on gobble-gobbling?'

'Never mind about that,' retorted Mrs. Judy. 'Do as you are told.'

So Judy lifted up the turkey and sat him down on the pink satin cushion. He trembled more than ever when he saw the enormous trumpet and wondered whether they were going to push him into it and do dreadful things to him, such as turning him into mince-meat, and he began to gobble at top speed. But after a few moments he felt better, because Judy was stroking his feathers very gently and Mrs. Judy was dabbing his tail with a piece of cotton wool dipped in rose-water, which was most soothing. He felt, quite rightly, that he had come among friends. So he just gobbled softly away to himself, wondering what would happen next.

Five minutes later Mrs. Judy gave a final turn to the handle which ran the clockwork motor, and drew a sheet of paper out of the Magic Typewriter

'I can't make head or tail of it,' she complained. 'Read that!'

She thrust the paper into Judy's hand. This was what Judy read . . .

WASHING. GREEN WATER.
BEHIND. VERY PRETTY LADY.
VERY BAD LADY. BEHIND HURTS.
PLEASE HELP. WASHING. VERY
PRETTY BAD LADY.

'What we have to find out is . . . who is the pretty lady?'

'Gobble—gobble—gobble,' cried the turkey.

'Quite, my dear,' said Mrs. Judy, patting its behind. 'But that doesn't get us very far. Because there seems also to be a very bad lady. And in the last line they're both mixed up together, which doesn't seem right at all.' She turned back to Judy. 'Wind up the motor again my dear, feed another feather into the trumpet and let's see what happens.'

But when she drew out the next sheet of paper all that was written on it was . . .

WASHING WASHING WASHING!
HELP!

At that moment there was a knock on the door and the local newspaper fell through the letter-box. Judy went to pick it up and then, as she laid it on the table, she happened to glance at the advertisement column. And she suddenly found herself reading the very same advertisement that had caught the eye of Miss Smith only a few days ago.

'Granny,' she cried, 'listen to this!'

When she had read it out Mrs. Judy merely shrugged her shoulders, and said that she didn't see why they should be interested in a laundry.

'But, Granny,' insisted Judy, 'Meadowstream is only away over the hill. And supposing the turkey didn't know the word for "laundry" he'd be sure to describe it as "washing".

While she was speaking the turkey began to jump up and down on the cushion in a state of great excitement.

Mrs. Judy sat up sharply. 'I believe you may be on the right track,' she agreed. 'But what about the very pretty lady and the very bad lady?'

Judy clapped her hands together. 'Don't you *see*? The laundry's been *sold*! And it was the very bad lady who bought it! And after she'd bought it, she did something terrible to the turkey who had to run away, and then . . .'

At this point the turkey began to gobble so loud and fast that her voice was drowned. Swiftly Mrs. Judy plucked out another feather and fed it into the machine, at the same time turning the handle to give more power to the motor. And when she drew out the piece of paper this was what was written on it . . .

TRUE! TRUE! TRUE!

Mrs. Judy stared at the message. She was so moved that there were tears in her eyes.

'Well, my dear,' she said at length, 'it looks as though my little invention is coming into its own.'

'But, Granny, what shall we *do*?'

The old lady threw back her head. She looked very proud and very fierce, as she always did when the happiness of an animal was at stake.

'Tomorrow,' she said, 'we go to Meadowstream!'

Chapter Four

As soon as Miss Smith had moved into the laundry, she stocked up the kitchen with all the disgusting things which she liked to have for dinner. If you had opened the door of her refrigerator you would have felt quite sick at the sight of them, such as rat sausages and jellied vipers. Perhaps the most distasteful of all these items was something she called 'caviar' which was, in fact, nothing but frogs' spawn. She collected it from stagnant ponds on the nights of the new moon, scooping it up with a shrimping-net and carrying it home in the skull of a dead goat. Then she poured it into the coldest compartment of the refrigerator and kept it to eat on specially happy occasions, such as funerals and railway accidents.

As soon as she had refreshed herself in this nasty way, she sat down in the drawing-room and went through the accounts of the laundry. What she discovered did not please her at all. The business was not making nearly enough money. But why? Miss Watkins—the lady from whom she had bought it—seemed to have worked quite hard, but she had hardly made a decent living, let alone a fortune. And Miss Smith was quite determined to make a fortune. She wanted to spend her old age in comfort, and since she was nearly four hundred, she felt that old age was only just around the corner.

So what was wrong? She studied the accounts more closely, and suddenly she had the answer. There were not enough customers! Too many people were doing their washing at home. Instead of bringing their linen to her laundry, they were stuffing it into their own wash-tubs and hanging it up to dry in their own back yards. Miss Smith felt that this was a very vulgar way of carrying on. Besides, it did not put a penny into her own pocket. These wretched people must be taught a lesson.

So she went into the kitchen to have a word with Beelzebub. He was sitting on the table nibbling caviar.

'Soda chonk?' asked Beelzebub, which means, of course, 'What do you want?'

She told him. As she spoke, his little red eyes glowed with excitement and his nose turned bright blue, which was always a sign that he was happy. And when Beelzebub was happy, it meant that somebody else would soon be very miserable indeed.

On the following morning Miss Smith began her wicked plan.

She dressed herself in her prettiest frock and stuck on her best pair of false eyelashes. Then she took a new wig out of the cupboard and placed Beelzebub gently on it, folding a golden curl over his back so that nobody would see him.

'Grog shootlepop,' observed Beelzebub as she put the wig on her head.

'Let us hope so,' rejoined Miss Smith. With which, she went outside, locking the door behind her.

She had scarcely walked a hundred yards before she found her first victim—an old lady who was hanging up the washing in the garden of a cottage covered with roses. As Miss Smith strolled towards her, she whispered to Beelzebub . . . 'Pocky tong Plop'. In Beetle Language this means: 'Get ready.'

Leaning over the fence she spoke in her sweetest tones

'Good morning, madam,' she said. 'My name is Miss Smith and I have just bought the little laundry in Green Street.'

The old lady merely sniffed and said, 'Nothing doing.'

Miss Smith was not used to being spoken to so rudely. However, she controlled herself.

She gave a silvery laugh. 'My *dear* madam,' she tinkled, 'I was only saying "good morning".'

'Well, you've said it,' observed the old lady, turning her back, 'and now you can go away.'

Miss Smith ground her teeth in anger. 'Klunk,' she hissed to Beelzebub. Which means 'Go into action'.

Aloud, she said . . . 'I hope you don't think that I was going to ask you to send your washing to *me*. Oh no! I could never wash things so white as *you* do.'

The old lady turned round. Miss Smith had said just the right thing. She was very proud of her washing and her heart began to melt.

'Well,' she muttered, 'I don't do it so badly.'

'Badly!' echoed Miss Smith. 'You do it quite beautifully!'

As she spoke she saw, out of the corner of her eye, that Beelzebub was working away at lightning speed. He had already spat two large red spots on to the drawers of the old lady's husband and sent a spurt of green slime on to her daughter's pyjamas. And now he was busy on her grandson's shorts, spitting purple fluid on the back, so that when he put them on he would look as though he had sat in something.

'*Quite* beautifully!' repeated Miss Smith. 'All the same, I do feel that there are one or two little things that you may not have noticed.'

The old lady looked surprised. 'What sort of things?'

'Things like spots.'

'Spots? There are never any spots on *my* washing!'

'No?' Miss Smith smiled even more sweetly. 'Then I expect it must be something to do with my eyesight. But I could have sworn that I saw one or two *tiny* little spots on your beautiful washing.'

As she spoke, Beelzebub flew swiftly back to nestle in her wig. At the same time, the old lady turned, and uttered a loud scream. A terrible sight met her eyes. Her washing had come out in a rash of spots and streaks and smudges.

'What has happened?' she cried.

Miss Smith shook her head sadly. 'I am afraid that you must be using the wrong washing powder.'

'But what sort of washing powder should I use?'

'Well,' said the witch, 'with spots like that I'm afraid that it would have to be something very special. Something like Witch-O.'

'But I've never heard of Witch-O,' exclaimed the old lady.

'Nobody has heard of it,' answered the witch. 'It is my special secret. In my laundry I use nothing else.' She turned as if to go. 'Well, madam,' she said with a charming smile, 'it has been such a pleasure to meet you. And I shouldn't worry too much about your washing. For all we know, your husband may be delighted to have his underwear covered in bright red spots. Men are such strange creatures, aren't they?'

'But he would not be at all delighted,' protested the old lady. 'He would be horrified. I must buy a packet of Witch-O at once.'

'That, madam, is quite impossible. Witch-O is not for sale.'

'Then whatever can I do?'

The witch appeared to be thinking the matter over. 'Well,' she said at length, 'I *might* be able to help you, as a special favour.'

'You mean, I should send my things to your laundry?'

'If you wish to have them properly done. Though, as I said before, it may not be necessary.' Her eyes wandered to the pair of shorts with the black smudges on the back. 'If your son is a really modern young man, he *might* think that those shorts were very smart. He might even take off his trousers to show them to his friends.'

'He would do no such thing,' protested the old lady. 'He is not at all a modern young man. He is very old-fashioned. He never takes off his trousers in public.'

'He sounds quite charming,' simpered the witch. 'But I really must be going now.'

The old lady put her hand on Miss Smith's arm. As she did so, she wondered why she felt a sudden chill, as though she had taken hold of an icicle. 'Please, please, take my things into your laundry.'

Miss Smith gave one of her silvery laughs. 'Oh dear me!' she said. 'How I get put upon! *Everybody* seems to want me to help them! Sometimes I wish that I hadn't got such a warm heart!'

The old lady could not help thinking that though Miss Smith's heart might be very warm, her arm was growing colder and colder. She drew her hand away.

'Then you will take my things?' she pleaded.

'Yes, madam, I will take them. And I will call for them this afternoon, at three o'clock.'

She blew the old lady a kiss and went on her way with a smile on her lips. As she turned the corner she felt a faint scratching in her wig. It was Beelzebub, who had been greatly enjoying himself during the past ten minutes.

She gave him an affectionate pat. 'Yes my darling? Had you anything to say?'

'Bum-bum,' observed Beelzebub. 'Pocky-pocky bum-bum'.

Miss Smith nodded graciously. 'That,' she said, 'is exactly what I was thinking myself.'

And now you will be wondering what had been happening to Snowdrop while all this had been going on.

Snowdrop was having a quite horrible time. In public, Miss Smith would smile sweetly at him and stroke him gently on the back to make people think that she loved him and would treat him kindly. But as soon as she reached the laundry, she always gave him a sharp slap and then she would hiss at him and cry, 'That will teach you, you horrible good creature. I hate you. You are so good that you make me feel quite ill.'

Snowdrop grew more and more bewildered. He did not know—as you and I know—that Miss Smith hated anything good. If he had been a *bad* pony, and if he had gone about biting babies and kicking old age pensioners she would have loved him dearly, and given him lumps of sugar and plenty of fresh straw and a green meadow to run about in. But there was not a single nasty thing about him; all he wanted was to be good, and to have a mistress whom he could love. And this was more than the witch could bear.

She and Beelzebub spent hours devising new tortures and torments. Never was Snowdrop more shocked than when Miss Smith, with a false show of kindness, offered him a handful of sugar lumps, his favourite treat. Rather greedily, it must be owned, he crunched them and swallowed; and suddenly his throat felt on fire and his stomach full of snakes. This was not surprising, considering that the sugar was made from the skins of rattlesnakes and the scales of cockroaches, ground together and mixed with the fins of whitings to give it the right colour.

Trembling with terror Snowdrop shuffled across the yard and stumbled into the dark narrow stable. He heard the door slam behind him and the key turning in the lock. Then he lay down and rested his head on a heap of dirty straw, with tears trickling down his face.

He felt utterly alone. Why had his mistress sold him to such a terrible person? What had he done to deserve such a fate?

Gradually, the pains grew less and he had a drink of water from a pail in the corner and a mouthful of the mixture which the witch had prepared for him in a bucket. The water was dirty and the mixture did not taste at all nice. However, at least it did not give him another pain and he found a grain of comfort from the thought that although Miss Smith might hate him she did not seem to want to kill him, at least not yet.

Blinking away his tears he hobbled over to the window which was the only source of light for his prison. It looked out into the back yard and over the wall he could just see a meadow in the distance, bathed in sunlight and golden with buttercups. The sight of it was almost too much for him, and he began to make sad little whinnying noises as though he were pleading for somebody to come and set him free. But then he was silent again, for he realized that if he were to make a noise the only person who would be able to hear him was the witch, and she might come in and slap him again, and perhaps she would make him swallow another of those horrible lumps of sugar. So he fought back his tears, gave a big gulp and went back to the corner to lie down and try to sleep.

Then, just as he was beginning to feel drowsy he heard a faint sound of scratching which seemed to come from the roof above. He looked up, but he could see nothing, so he struggled to his feet and peered into the semi-darkness. To his astonishment he saw that the scratching came from a white mouse who was nibbling away at the beam like mad as though it were a piece of chocolate. His first instinct was to mistrust this curious creature; she might be in the pay of the witch and have been sent to spy on him. But as he looked more closely, his fears began to vanish because the mouse looked so very harmless. Her tail flicked backwards and forwards, as though it were waving a signal of welcome, and now and then she turned her head, sat on her hind legs and gave a friendly wink. So Snowdrop went closer and asked her who she was and what she was up to.

To his surprise, the mouse made no reply. She only sighed and shook her head. If only we could have borrowed Mrs. Judy's Animal Translator we should have been able to tell you exactly what the pony said on this occasion, but unfortunately Mrs. Judy very seldom lends it to people. However, we can give you the rough idea. It went something like this:

Snowdrop: What are you doing up there?
Mouse: No reply.
Snowdrop: Are you a friend of Miss Smith?
Mouse: Shakes head violently.
Snowdrop: Are you trying to help me?
Mouse: Nods several times.
Snowdrop: But how can you help me by eating away at that old beam?
Mouse: No reply.
Snowdrop: Anyway, why won't you speak to me?
Mouse: No reply.
Snowdrop: Can't you even tell me your name?

When he asked her this question the mouse nodded again, reached behind her and drew out a little card which she held between her teeth. Snowdrop craned his neck to see what was written on it. This was what he read . . .

DUMBELLE

So that was it . . . the mouse was dumb!

'I am terribly sorry,' said Snowdrop. And indeed he was, for he had the kindest of hearts. He was also sorry on his own account. It would have been a comfort to have somebody to talk to, even somebody so small and squeaky. But no, 'Squeaky' was not all the right word, because she could not give even the smallest of squeaks; she could make no sound of any sort.

'I am terribly sorry,' repeated Snowdrop. And then, as conversation seemed to have come to a full stop, he went back to his corner, lay down and closed his eyes. There were all sorts of other questions he would have liked to put to Dumbelle, but what was the use? All the same, he did feel a little better for her company and when he went to sleep he comforted himself by the thought that he was no longer completely alone. He had *one* friend, even if she was a very small one.

So he slept, while Dumbelle went back to nibbling the beam. 'Nibble, nibble, nibble . . . scratch, scratch, scratch. Pause.' Then again . . . 'Scratch, scratch, scratch . . . nibble, nibble, nibble.' Pause.

And at this point, we might also pause to ask ourselves a question. Supposing a very small mouse starts to nibble a very big beam, what happens? Well, gradually the beam will be nibbled right through. And then? The beam will fall, and the roof will cave in, and the walls fall down, and Snowdrop will be able to escape from his prison.

Yes, you may reply, but it may be years before that happens. That may be true. But we must not forget that Dumbelle's teeth are very sharp and her heart is very brave—and with a brave heart, whether you are a mouse or a man, you may sometimes work wonders, even if you only do a little at a time.

Chapter Five

'*Tomorrow*,' *Mrs. Judy had said when we last met her* '*we will* go to Meadowstream!'

But on the following morning she tripped over a root of the tree and sprained her ankle. It was so painful that she had to stay in bed.

'But there is no reason why *you* shouldn't go,' she said to her grand-daughter.

'But Granny, I don't like leaving you alone.'

'Stuff and nonsense! I can look after myself. Besides I shan't be alone. I shall have the turkey to look after me. You know, my dear, I'm becoming quite attached to that odd creature.'

Judy smiled and looked over towards the turkey, who was strutting up and down the meadow, gobbling softly to himself.

'He certainly is odd,' she agreed. 'But he doesn't seem unhappy any more. Instead of being ashamed of those feathers he looks quite proud of them.'

'That was *my* doing,' said Mrs. Judy. 'When you went out last night to fetch the milk, I did some hard thinking. At first I decided I ought to cut his feathers off, but I was afraid of hurting him. Then I thought I might perhaps do it by magic. However . . . 'she shook her head and sighed . . . 'I'm not so good at magic as I used to be. I'm growing old.'

'Don't be silly, Granny. You'll never be old.'

Mrs. Judy patted her hand affectionately. 'It's kind of you to say so, dear, but I'm very old indeed, and at my age one's supply of magic is limited. And it seemed foolish to waste any of it on a little matter like a turkey's tail. I may soon be needing all my magic for much more important affairs.'

'So what did you do?'

'The first thing I did was to give him a name. Nobody had ever called him anything but "turkey" before. I thought that if he only had a name it would help him to get back his self-respect.'

'What name did you give him?'

'Chirutrotskey.'

Judy looked puzzled. 'Doesn't that sound rather Russian?'

'Of course it sounds Russian,' retorted her grandmother. 'It also sounds very aristocratic. It might be the name of a Russian prince.'

Judy nodded. 'Yes, it might. All the same I don't quite see why you chose such a very long name.'

The old lady gave an impatient snort. 'You are being very dense. How do you spell ostrich and turkey?'

'O-S-T-R-I-C-H and T-U-R-K-E-Y.'

'Correct. Now put those thirteen letters together, mix them all up and what do you get?'

Judy thought for a moment. 'Why—you get Chirutrotskey!'

'Of course, though you took rather a long time to see it.'

'I shall call him Trotsky for short,' said Judy.

'It doesn't matter what you call him. What matters is that when I sat him in front of the Translator and explained it to him, he was obviously very pleased.'

'Did you tell him anything else?'

'Yes. I told him that he was a great big silly bird to be so ashamed, and that lots of turkeys would be proud to have such wonderful feathers.'

'And did he believe you?'

'He did. If you doubt it, look at him now.'

Judy looked again towards the turkey and realized that her grandmother was right. The turkey was strutting up and down as proud as a peacock. From time to time, he glanced over his shoulder, spread his feathers, shook himself and said, 'Gobble—gobble—gobble.' We have heard him say that before, but not in the same tone of voice. His 'Gobble—gobble—gobble' was no longer a cry of pain or fear. It was a very happy sound indeed.

'Darling Trotsky,' laughed Judy. 'I feel that he's become quite one of the family.'

Her granny nodded. 'So he has. The only thing I'm afraid of is that I may have made him too conceited.'

In spite of Mrs. Judy's protestations it was not until three days later that Judy decided she was well enough to be left alone. This delay was unfortunate, because it gave the witch just the time she needed to settle down and to work out her plans. It also gave her time to get Snowdrop completely into her clutches. There was no longer a chance that he might break free from her; his spirit was broken. He dared not even cry when she was around, for if she saw so much as a tear in his eye, she started slapping him and calling him awful names. 'How dare you look so miserable, you wretched creature?' she would hiss at him. 'What will people think? Hold your head up! Lift up your feet! And when you look at me, look as though you loved me. If you don't I shall cut off your tail and make you eat it for supper.'

Poor Snowdrop was terrified by this threat, as well he might be, for he knew that the witch was quite capable of doing such a thing. So he swallowed his tears, held back his head, lifted up his feet and tried to look cheerful. What else could he do in the circumstances?

And that was how Judy saw Snowdrop, when she first met him; a beautiful pony, plump and glistening white, holding his head high and glancing back at his mistress, as though she were the person he loved most in the world.

On the outskirts of Meadowstream Judy had paused, to decide on a plan of action.

She was a bright little girl, and she was not only bright but brave. However she had to admit that she had no real notion of what to do, nor how to do it. All she had to go on was the strange message which Trotsky had gobbled into Mrs. Judy's Translator.

She sat down under an old elm tree and put her thoughts into words. 'It's like one of those detective stories,' she said to herself, 'and if I'm going to solve it I must try to understand the clues. What *are* they? Well, first there's Trotsky, who ran away from the laundry where he was ill-treated by somebody he calls the Very Bad Lady. I think we can be fairly certain that it *was* a laundry. He never actually used the word, and only talked about "Washing". But when he was gobbling into the Translator and when he heard us talking about the laundry, he jumped up and down and said "True". So the first thing I must do is to go there and see what sort of place it is.'

'But that's only the beginning,' she reflected. 'Who *is* the Very Bad Lady and how am I to know that she is so bad? If she is as bad as Trotsky says, she isn't likely to let people know it. She probably pretends to be very good. She may even be wearing some sort of disguise. The only thing I can be sure about is that there is also a Very Pretty

Lady, and I do hope that she is the one I shall meet first. She sounds a very sweet sort of person, and she may be able to tell me what it is all about.'

Judy shook her head in bewilderment. It was all very difficult. At the same time it was also very exciting, like all the best detective stories. So she got up from under the elm tree and hurried on her way to the village.

Twenty minutes later Judy was standing outside the laundry ringing the bell. While she was waiting she stood on tip-toe to look over the hedge into the garden. What a pretty little house it was! Not like a laundry at all . . . more like a village shop where they sold acid-drops and ice-cream. However, it must be the right place, because of the notice that was nailed on the door.

MEADOWSTREAM LAUNDRY LTD.
Under entirely new Management
Exclusive to this Establishment
WITCH-O
The Whitest Washer in The World
Proprietress
MISS SMITH

But why did nobody answer the bell? She began to feel impatient and rang again.

Then she heard footsteps coming towards her. Turning round she saw an old lady wheeling a big bundle of washing in a perambulator. It was Mrs. Greenapple, who, you may remember, had been the witch's first customer.

'Nobody at home?' she enquired. 'Then Miss Smith must still be making her rounds.'

'Will she be back soon?'

'She should be. But she's so popular that she may have

been delayed. Everybody wants to talk to her because she's so pretty.'

Judy's heart began to beat faster. It looked as though she had found at least one of the people whom she had been seeking.

'Is she really very pretty?' she asked.

'Quite beautiful', the old lady assured her. 'And as good as she is beautiful. Wait till you see Snowdrop her little pony. He's very white and fat and he adores her.'

She unloaded her bundle of washing, piled it on the doorstep and sat down on it. She was a lonely old person and glad of somebody to talk to. Judy was only too happy to let her rattle on; the more she could learn about Miss Smith, the better.

'Yes,' continued Mrs. Greenapple, 'she is a most charming girl. And yet . . .' For a moment she hesitated.

'Yes?' prompted Judy.

'Well, my dear, perhaps I shouldn't say it, but sometimes I feel there's something rather strange about her.'

'Strange?'

'Yes. For instance, why does she only do her washing in the middle of the night?'

'Perhaps it's because she spends all the day going round to collect it,' suggested Judy.

'That's what I thought at first. But then, you see, she never turns the lights on. She does it all in the dark.'

'In the dark?' Judy looked astonished. 'Are you sure?'

'Quite sure. I've seen her. I'm a very bad sleeper, and sometimes I get out of bed and go for walks in the moonlight. And last week I walked down this very street and stopped outside this very house. Though it was long after midnight, the washing machines were working away like mad, and there was Miss Smith, putting piles of linen into them.'

'But how could you see her if there were no lights?'

'That's the strangest thing of all,' exclaimed the old lady. 'There *were* lights. But they didn't come from the electricity. They came from the water she was washing the things in. It was a sort of greenish glow, very pale and flickering, and it rather frightened me. Miss Smith looked somehow . . . different. Not nearly so pretty and much older. The whole thing made me think of ghosts.'

Judy smiled. 'I don't believe in ghosts,' she said. 'There was probably a quite simple explanation. It may have been something she put in the water.'

Mrs. Greenapple returned her smile. 'You're a clever little girl. It *was* something she put in the water. She said so herself on the following morning. When I told her about having seen through the window she looked quite cross for a moment, as though she thought I'd been spying. Then she gave one of her laughs and said, "Oh Mrs. Greenapple, you've found out my little secret! You've actually seen Witch-O at work! And now you know how splendid it is! It makes its own light as soon as I put it into the water, and that's why I always do my washing in the dark!" '

'She sounds a wonderful person,' said Judy.

'She is indeed. And I really am devoted to her. It's just that she's . . . I don't know how to put it . . . she's *different*.'

'In what way?'

For a moment the old lady did not answer. Then she asked Judy a very curious question. 'Are you, by any chance, fond of bats?'

'Bats?' The very thought of them made Judy shudder. '*Bats*?' she echoed. 'Oh no! They're the most horrible creatures! They fly about at night, and they squeak and they put their claws in people's hair.'

'Quite so,' assented the old lady gravely. 'And once they have got their claws in they never let go. They hang on like limpets and the only way to get rid of them is to have all your hair cut off. I could never grow really fond of a bat.'

'Neither could I,' agreed Judy. 'But why did you mention them?'

'Because Miss Smith *is* very fond of them.'

'Miss Smith? Surely not!'

The old lady sighed. 'Perhaps I am doing her an injustice,' she said. 'Perhaps it isn't Miss Smith who is so fond of the bats. Perhaps it's the other way round. Perhaps it's the bats who are so fond of *her*.'

'I'm afraid I don't understand,' said Judy.

'You'd have understood if you'd been with me the other night,' retorted Mrs. Greenapple. 'D'you see that tree over there?' She pointed to an old apple tree in the yard. 'It was covered with bats—covered with them! And so was the oak, and the weeping willow! There were hundreds and hundreds of them.'

Judy began to feel quite frightened, and her voice was trembling when she spoke again. 'What were the bats doing?'

'They were looking.'

'Looking at what?'

'At Miss Smith.' She put out a skinny hand and clutched Judy's arm. 'They were all looking at her with their terrible little yellow eyes, sitting on the branches, staring through the windows. And . . . and . . .'

'And what?'

The old lady's voice sunk to a whisper. 'They were looking at her as though they loved her!'

Poor Judy felt bewildered. For a moment she wondered whether Mrs. Greenapple might be mad. But she had spoken with such conviction that she must be telling the truth.

But what did it all mean? Why should Miss Smith have this strange attraction for bats? A whole lot of other questions whirled around in her head. Why did Miss Smith do her washing in the dark? Why didn't she turn on the lights? Why didn't she open the windows and scream and shoo the bats away?

She would dearly have liked to ask these questions, but she had no time to do so for at that moment there was a clatter of hoofs at the end of the lane and Miss Smith came into view, driving her laundry cart. She looked so beautiful, with her golden hair and her long eyelashes, and Snowdrop looked so white and happy, that Judy's heart went out to her. 'Here,' she thought, 'is somebody I could really love.'

Chapter Six

When Miss Smith saw Judy on the doorstep she was very angry. A single glance was enough to tell her that Judy was a good little girl and, in her opinion, there ought to be a law against good little girls.

For a moment she felt like galloping away and giving the whole thing up. She had spent a dreadful morning, chatting to dozens of people who were all very good, and pretending to like them. She was feeling extremely lonely, with nobody of her own sort to talk to. If only she could have a chat with a nice little girl who had just murdered her aunt, or a nice little boy who had just robbed a bank or hi-jacked an aeroplane she would have felt more at peace with the world. But no such pleasant people had come her way.

However, she had to put a brave face on it, so she advanced towards Mrs. Greenapple with a glowing smile. 'How delightful to see you!' she exclaimed. 'More washing? Splendid! I will bring it back to you tomorrow. And who is this dear little person? Judy? What a pretty name! And what can I do for you, Judy?'

Judy was rather taken aback by this question because she was not at all sure what Miss Smith could do for her. So she pretended that she had not heard.

'What a beautiful pony!' she said to Miss Smith.

'Yes, isn't he,' agreed the witch enthusiastically.

'May I give him a lump of sugar?'

'Of course. There's nothing he loves so much.'

Judy took a lump from her pocket and held it out to Snowdrop. To her surprise he shied away. 'He doesn't seem to want it,' she said to the witch.

'Not want it? How very odd! I wonder why?'

This was, of course, quite untrue; Miss Smith knew very well the reason for Snowdrop's behaviour; he was afraid that the sugar would give him another pain. Ever since that first lump, he had a horror of the very sight of it. How was he to know that the lump Judy was offering him was wholesome and sweet? He had lost his faith in humans; he had come to believe that they were all as bad as the witch. And yet, as he stared at Judy, he wondered whether she might not perhaps be somebody he could trust. For a moment he toyed with the idea of accepting the sugar and he licked his lips, for he was very hungry. Then he thought better of it and shied away again.

Miss Smith stepped forward, smiling gaily. 'Naughty Snowdrop,' she murmured. 'I think I know why he doesn't want it. He's been stealing from my kitchen again, haven't you my sweet?' She gave him a playful slap. Turning to Judy she said, 'I haven't the heart to punish him, but I'll just take him out to his meadow, because if he's stolen as much sugar as he usually does, the poor darling may not be feeling very well.'

Whereupon she led Snowdrop out to the meadow, closing the gate behind her. A few minutes later she was back again. 'How kind she is,' thought Judy as she watched her helping Mrs. Greenapple to lift her heavy load of laundry. And when the old lady had gone, and when she was left with Miss Smith alone, she thought she had seldom seen anybody so beautiful.

And yet . . . there *was* something strange about her. Something she could not put into words.

'And now,' enquired the witch, 'what can I do for you, my dear? Is it about something to be washed?'

'No. It's not quite like that. I wonder . . . I mean . . . would you mind if we went indoors for a minute?'

'Not at all.' Miss Smith was only too glad to take Judy into her cottage, for she had designed it as a sort of show piece, to put people off the scent and make them think how good and virtuous she was. Which was what Judy thought when she stepped into the parlour.

It was a pretty room and you could see at a glance that it belonged to somebody with high moral standards. Over the fireplace was a large photograph of St. Paul's Cathedral which was obviously a good sign. On the opposite wall hung several pictures of saints, with haloes round their heads. In a bowl on the table there was a lovely pile of pot-pourri, made from rose petals, which gave out an enchanting perfume.

'It's quite beautiful,' murmured Judy, gazing around her.

'Very simple, I'm afraid,' replied the witch. 'Nothing valuable. Just a few of the things I love.'

Had Judy only known, this was a shameless lie, because Miss Smith hated all these things. The pictures were only hung up to deceive people. Every night, when there was no danger of anybody walking in, Miss Smith turned them round with their faces to the wall. And then you would have seen what she really did love, for on the other side of St. Paul's Cathedral she had pasted a picture of Hell, drawn from memory by another witch who had actually spent a weekend there. On the back of the portraits of the saints there were hideous likenesses of demons and devils. And instead of the bowl of pot-pourri, there was an evil-smelling mixture of dead blow-flies and rancid cheese.

Judy could not guess these things. Although she still

felt that there was something strange about Miss Smith, she had to admit that she seemed a very good person, who was evidently very fond of religion.

'And now,' said the witch averting her eyes from the picture of St. Paul's, which was apt to give her a headache, 'what was it that you wished to tell me?'

'I'm afraid you will think it rather peculiar,' replied Judy, 'but it's about a turkey.'

'A turkey?' echoed Miss Smith. She spoke with genuine astonishment, for she had completely forgotten about Trotsky. 'What sort of turkey?'

'Well,' said Judy, 'it has ostrich feathers coming out of its behind.'

A gleam of understanding came into Miss Smith's eye; she scented danger. But she was too cunning to show it, so she gave one of her silvery laughs.

'How amusing,' she tinkled. 'Whoever heard of such a creature? It must look quite unusual.'

'It does indeed, and we can't understand how it happened.'

'We?' The witch spoke sharply. 'Who do you mean by "we"?'

'Myself and my grandmother. You see, the turkey was running away, and we found him—and we were so sorry for him that we gave him a home.'

'How kind of you,' smiled the witch. 'But what has all this got to do with *me*?'

'It really hasn't anything to do with you at all,' began Judy. 'It's only that . . .'

'Yes?'

And then Judy paused, for she could have sworn that she saw a puff of green smoke floating out of Miss Smith's nostrils. 'Obviously,' she said to herself, 'I must be mistaken. Miss Smith is not smoking, and even if she were it would not make green smoke come out of her nose. However, it makes one think.'

'Yes?' repeated the witch, dabbing her nose with a lace handkerchief. She was beginning to hate this tiresome little girl more than ever.

Judy still hesitated. She had been about to tell Miss Smith the whole story—how Trotsky had come to them, how he had sat down in front of the Translator and gobbled into it, and told them about the Very Bad Lady and the Very Pretty Lady. Suddenly she felt unsure. Miss Smith was certainly very beautiful and she must also be very good. But was she to be trusted?

'Yes?' repeated the witch for the third time. 'You still haven't told me what all this has to do with me.'

Judy made up her mind. 'No,' she said to herself, 'I shall not tell her. Not until I've spoken to Granny.'

So she merely said, 'Everybody says how kind you are. So I thought you might be able to help. Particularly as you keep poultry yourself.'

'Not turkeys,' retorted Miss Smith quickly. 'And certainly not turkeys with ostrich feathers coming out of their behinds. I wouldn't allow such creatures near the house.'

She spoke with heat because she was beginning to feel very worried by this tiresome little girl. Not only because she was good—but because she was nosey, and if there was one thing she hated, it was noseyness. When you are a witch you have to avoid nosey people like the plague, because they are apt to find out your secrets. And it was obvious that Judy had already found out one of her secrets, in the shape of the turkey. Apart from that, there was Snowdrop. The witch suspected that Judy had taken a fancy to Snowdrop, and if she were to discover about *him*, there would be no end of trouble.

Yes, Miss Smith was very worried indeed. However, she managed to control herself.

'Well, my dear,' she said at length, 'it is all very difficult and I only wish that I could help you.' She sighed pathetically. Then a sudden thought occurred to her. 'At the same time,' she said, 'perhaps there *is* something that I could do. I could come over to your house and examine the poor thing.'

'Examine it?'

'Well . . . get to know it. One can't help unless one knows all the facts can one? So will you please give me your address?'

Judy did not know what to do. She had a feeling that her granny would not like Miss Smith, but she also felt that it would be rude to refuse to tell Miss Smith where she lived. So she wrote down the address of the House Under the Tree, and drew a rough map showing the winding paths that led towards it.

The witch took the map and folded it into her bag. As she did so, Beelzebub flew in from the garden and fluttered on to the window-ledge, where he sat staring at her with his bright green eyes.

'Heavens,' cried Judy. 'What an enormous beetle!'

Miss Smith turned round with a start. Beelzebub was the last person she would have wished to arrive at this moment. On the rare occasions when he appeared he always made a bad impression. She frowned at him and hissed a single word—'Kronkpot'—which of course means 'Go away.'

Aloud, she exclaimed . . . 'Beetle?' She looked to the left and to the right and up to the ceiling—everywhere but to the window-ledge. 'Where is it?'

'Straight in front of you,' replied Judy impatiently.

Miss Smith was now obliged to turn towards Beelzebub

'Oh, I see what you mean,' she laughed, 'you mean that beautiful butterfly!' At the same time she shook her head at him and again she hissed, 'Kronkpot!'

Beelzebub had been so well trained that he usually did exactly as he was told. For once in a while he was tempted to disobey. He did not want to Kronkpot at all. There was something about Judy that appealed to him, in some strange way that he did not understand. But when the witch hissed 'Kronkpot' for the third time he reluctantly opened his wings and flew back into the gardens.

'Was it really a butterfly?' asked Judy doubtfully. 'It looked much more like a beetle to me. How can you be sure?'

The witch was longing to scratch Judy's eyes out, but she controlled herself. 'Because, my dear, I happen to know a great deal about butterflies,' she replied. 'In fact, I have written a book about them.'

She spoke so sweetly, and so earnestly, that Judy believed her.

'Have you really?' she enquired. 'Could I read it?'

'No, my dear. I am afraid that it is out of print.'

Judy sighed. 'I should have loved to read a book about butterflies.' Then she said, 'And please, Miss Smith, what does "Kronkpot" mean?'

The witch, clenching her fists and grinding her teeth, still managed to keep a smile on her face. 'It is the *name* of the butterfly, my dear. Very rare in this country. There are two sorts, the Greater Kronkpot and the Lesser Kronkpot. The butterfly you saw was one of the Greater Kronkpots. The reason people so seldom see them is because they are usually very frightened of human beings.'

Judy was much impressed. 'Well, at any rate,' she said, 'this one wasn't frightened of *you*.'

'Nobody is ever frightened of little me,' laughed Miss

Smith. She rose to her feet. 'Well, my dear,' she said, 'it has been such a pleasure to meet you. And now, if you will excuse me . . .'

As she spoke, there was the sound of a motor-horn outside. She glanced out of the window and exclaimed, 'Gracious me, it is the Duchess.'

'Which Duchess?' enquired Judy.

'The Duchess of Meadowstream, my dear,' replied the witch breathlessly. 'Such a charming woman! She lives in an enormous house with eighty bedrooms and I believe she has come to give me all her laundry to wash.' She darted over to the mirror and dabbed her nose with a powder puff. She was obviously in a state of great excitement. Turning to Judy she said, 'You will understand, my dear, if I ask you to leave? And perhaps it would be best if you went by the back door.'

Before she knew what was happening, Judy found herself being pushed out of the cottage, and though she was only a small girl in shabby clothes she could not help feeling that Miss Smith had dismissed her rather abruptly.

However, as she looked over her shoulder towards the waiting motor-car, she understood that Miss Smith could not really have introduced her to the Duchess. She had never met a duchess, but this was obviously an extra special one. She had a big hook nose and a very haughty expression and she wore a huge diamond tiara on top of her head. On the panels of the motor-car there was a coat of arms in bright gold, and there was also a lot of gold braid on her chauffeur's uniform.

Miss Smith swept her a low curtsey and from the distance Judy heard the Duchess speak. She had a very duchessy sort of voice.

'My deah Miss Smith,' she said. 'Such a pleasuah! I have come to welcome you to our little village.'

Whereupon Miss Smith curtseyed for a second time and murmured that she was honoured.

'Not at all, my deah gal,' replied the Duchess. 'But there is also a matter of business. I am having a few people to stay the weekend—seventy-five to be precise—and my maid tells me that there will be a hundred and fifty pairs of sheets to wash, and she seems to think that this is too much for her to manage single-handed. Could you help me?'

The witch curtseyed once more.

'Splendid, my deah! We will drive to the Castle at once.' She motioned Miss Smith to sit beside her and a moment later they were on their way. The car made a great deal of dust, but the Duchess's tiara was so bright that Judy could see it sparkling into the far distance.

Suddenly, she felt tired. She had spent a busy day and seen a great many unusual things, and she wanted to go home to granny and talk about them. On the way, she paused at the village shop to buy some chocolate fudge. The taste of it reminded her of Snowdrop, and again she asked herself why he had refused her lump of sugar. Was it really because he had been stealing from Miss Smith? He did not look that sort of pony at all, in which case she must have been telling an untruth. But *she* did not look like that sort of person either.

And then . . . the beetle. She could have sworn that it *was* a beetle, but Miss Smith had been equally certain that it was a butterfly. And Miss Smith had written a book about butterflies.

Dear me, what a lot there was to think about, and what a lot of questions there were to ask!

Chapter Seven

'*D*uchesses!'

It was Mrs. Judy speaking an hour later, when Judy had returned to the House Under the Tree, and when they were having supper together.

'Duchesses!' she repeated, in even more scornful tones. 'Who wants duchesses?'

'But there was only one Duchess, Granny darling. And she had only come about the washing.'

'I don't care why she had come. But it isn't the Duchess I'm bothered about. There are lots of other things. There's the green smoke coming out of that woman's nose.'

'Perhaps I was wrong. Perhaps I only thought I saw it.'

'How can you talk such rubbish? Have you ever seen green smoke coming out of *my* nose? Have you ever seen green smoke coming out of anybody's nose? No, you have not. You know, of course, what it means?'

Judy shook her head.

'It means . . . witches!'

Judy could scarcely believe her ears. 'How could Miss Smith possibly be a witch? She's so beautiful.'

'Considering all I've spent on your education,' snapped Mrs. Judy, 'you're sadly ignorant. Sometimes I wonder what they teach you at school. Any child ought to know at least *something* about witches. And the first thing you should have learnt is that the beautiful ones are much worse than the ugly ones. Much scarcer too.'

She gave a snort and began to fan herself with her hat.

In a calmer voice she went on . . . 'I'm sorry, my dear, if I seem irritable. But I don't like this hot weather, and there's a lot about this whole business that I don't understand. Are you *sure* about that pony and the sugar?'

'Quite. He wouldn't touch it. He was frightened of something.'

'And yet he was plump? And his coat was glossy?'

'Yes. He looked perfectly well. Perhaps I was wrong.'

'My dear, you are talking nonsense again. You're never wrong about animals. You mayn't be good at arithmetic, but when it comes to animals, you're first-rate. In fact, your'e even better than I am.'

'Oh, Granny, how can you say such things? Think of your Translator! You can even read their language.'

'Yes, my dear. But you seem to be able to read their thoughts, which is better still.'

Judy had a sudden idea. 'Couldn't we call Trotsky and get him to gobble into the Translator and tell us what he thinks of it?'

'We could, but it wouldn't be any use. The silly bird has gone and got himself a sore throat, and can hardly gobble at all.' She turned her head and called out to Trotsky, who was sitting in the shadow of the hedge, looking very sad. 'Come here, Trotsky,' she cried, 'and let's have a look at you!'

Trotsky waddled towards them. His feathers were bedraggled and trailed behind him in the long grass. His throat was bright red and swollen. He was the most miserable looking turkey you ever saw.

Judy patted him, smoothed his feathers and tried to make them stand up. But they only fell back into the grass.

'Poor Trotsky!' she murmured. 'Isn't there *anything* you can tell us?'

Trotsky looked up at her pathetically, swallowed and tried to gobble. But all he could manage was a sort of hiccup.

Mrs. Judy sighed. 'It's too tiresome. Everything seems to be going wrong today. I think I shall go back into the tree and lie down.'

Judy did not try to stop her. She thought that it was high time her granny stopped going up the tree at all, but if she had said so the old lady would have only climbed right to the top, out of sheer obstinacy.

In the meantime the witch made yet another friend, to whom we shall shortly be introduced. But first we must tell you how she met him.

It was at Meadowstream Castle where, as you may remember, the Duchess took Miss Smith when she called at the laundry. The witch played her cards so well and was so completely charming that by the time they arrived at the Castle the Duchess had quite fallen in love with her and asked her to stay to luncheon.

You may think it odd for a Duchess to ask a washerwoman to luncheon, but she was a very advanced sort of Duchess, so the Duke was not at all surprised when he saw her walking into the dining-room. Besides, she looked so beautiful with her golden hair and her long false eyelashes that he did not care what she might do in private life.

They drank white wine out of silver goblets and ate caviar off golden plates. Miss Smith had some difficulty in eating the caviar because she would greatly have preferred frog spawn, but she concealed her distaste and swallowed it with an effort. After the caviar they had lobsters and then they had vanilla ice-cream with cherries on the top.

When they had finished the Duchess turned to Miss Smith and said, 'Are you fond of horses, my deah gal?'

'Oh yes indeed,' replied the witch. 'There is nothing I love more than a nice horse.'

The Duchess nodded approvingly. 'I thought so as soon as I saw your beautiful pony. What did you say his name was?'

'Snowdrop.'

'Such a pretty name. And has he a sweet nature, too?'

'He has *now*,' lied the witch, 'but when he first came he was quite wicked.'

'But what did he do?'

'He kicked and bit and would never eat his dinner.'

'You don't say so. And how did you cure him?'

'Simply by love, my dear Duchess. You see, he had never been really loved before. When he saw how much I loved him, he changed his ways.'

It would have served the witch right if she had choked while she was uttering these falsehoods, but they fell from her lips like honey, and the Duchess was greatly impressed.

'You may wonder why I am asking you these questions,' she said. 'It is because one of our own horses is giving us a great deal of trouble.'

'What is his name?'

The question was answered by the Duke. 'We,' he growled, 'call him Satan!'

When she heard the name of the Devil, a gleam came into the witch's eyes. 'What a beautiful name!' she exclaimed. Then she hastily corrected herself. 'I mean, what a terrible name!'

'Not terrible enough, if you ask me,' retorted the Duke. 'Never knew such a horse. Nobody dares go near him.'

Miss Smith put on a saintly expression. 'Perhaps he has not had enough love,' she suggested.

'Pshaw! How can you love a brute whose one idea is to bite you? The worst part of it, Miss Smith, is that he's the finest horse in the whole stables. If only he were properly trained he'd be worth a fortune.'

A wicked plan began to form in the witch's brain, but she kept her angelic expression. 'Dear me,' she sighed 'it all sounds very difficult . . . and you say that he might be worth a fortune?'

'There isn't a race in the world that he wouldn't win. But where are we to find the right person to train him?'

Miss Smith's expression became more angelic than ever. 'I wonder,' she whispered, 'if the right person might be . . . myself?'

An hour later, Miss Smith had it all in the bag.

After luncheon, they had gone out to the stables to inspect the horses. Miss Smith hated horses, and if Beelzebub had been with her she would have sent him off to sting their noses. But when she saw Satan she realized that here was a horse that she could love; he was obviously the wickedest horse in the world.

He was kept apart from the others in a special stable. He was to dangerous to go near them, and his language was shocking; even the toughest old stallions used to say that they had never heard the like. It was lucky that the Duchess could not understand it; she would have had him removed at once. Miss Smith, needless to say, understood it very well, and greatly enjoyed it.

'So this is Satan!' she exclaimed, walking towards him.

The Duke put his hand on her arm. 'Don't go too close!' he urged. As he spoke he wondered why his fingers felt suddenly so cold.

The witch brushed him aside, saying with a laugh that

she was not in the least afraid of Satan. Then she walked ahead, and as soon as she was close enough she muttered a few phrases in witch language which had an extraordinary effect. He stopped champing his teeth and stamping his hoofs. He stayed still and the wild light faded from his eyes. Then he put his head out to be patted, gazing at Miss Smith with a look of devotion.

'This is the strangest thing,' whispered the Duchess.

'Never seen anything like it,' agreed the Duke. 'He looks as if he'd eat out of her hand.'

'He *is* eating out of her hand.' And indeed he was, for the witch had taken a piece of sugar from her bag, and Satan was crunching it hungrily. It was the same sort of sugar that had given Snowdrop such a pain, but she knew that it would not give Satan a pain. He was far too wicked.

Miss Smith walked back to them, smiling sweetly. 'Well, Duchess,' she observed, 'he seems quite a dear. I can't think why you found him so difficult.'

'Difficult? He was diabolical,' growled the Duke. 'But now . . . I don't know what to think. What is your secret, young lady?'

Miss Smith murmured that she had no secret at all, and that it was all a matter of love. Just plain, simple love. With which she turned to go, blowing Satan a farewell kiss.

The effect on Satan was immediate. As soon as he saw her going he let out a blood-curdling neigh, and leapt up and down on the floor of his stall with great specks of yellow foam coming out of his mouth.

'Heavens!' cried the Duchess. 'He's worse than ever! What on earth are we to do?'

Miss Smith shrugged her shoulders.

'Look out!' shouted the Duke. 'He's trying to escape from his stall!'

True enough, Satan was crashing at the barrier with

his hoofs and tearing at the door with his huge yellow teeth.

'Leave him to me,' said Miss Smith gently. She turned round once again and this time she gave Satan a wink. A long, wicked wink that told him all he wanted to know. It told him that she was his friend, that she had come to rescue him and that he must leave it all to her. Whereupon he gave quite a different sort of neigh, soft and peaceful, and retired to his stall.

As soon as they returned to the Castle, the Duchess sank into a chair, removed her tiara and called for a glass of brandy, observing that she felt quite shattered. 'And what we should have done without you, my deah,' she said to the witch. 'I really do not know. Thank heavens you were there.'

'Quite,' agreed the Duke. 'But Miss Smith will not always be with us. What shall we do about Satan when she is gone?'

An idea occurred to the Duchess and she leant forward eagerly. 'My deah gal ... *must* you go? Could you not come and stay with us?'

The Duke nodded. 'Meadowstream Castle will always be open to you, my dear!'

Miss Smith shook her head, and sighed that it was too kind of them, but she was just a simple girl who would feel out of place in a great big castle. Besides, who would take care of her little laundry?

'If it comes to that,' demanded the Duke, 'who will take care of Satan?'

The witch looked innocently up to the ceiling. 'Of course, if it would really help you, I could give him a home myself.'

The Duchess clapped her hands in delight. 'You would?'

'I only want to help,' repeated the witch. 'If you care for the idea, that is to say.'

'Care for it?' The Duke seemed equally delighted. 'It would solve everything!' Then he frowned 'But how will you get him home?'

'I shall ride him,' she replied simply.

The thought of this sweet, fragile girl with the golden hair and the fluttering eyelashes, getting on to the back of such a terrible beast as Satan and riding away with him was almost too much for the Duchess, and it was quite a long while before she allowed herself to be persuaded.

But finally it was all settled, and they went out into the great hall to make their farewells. 'There is no need for anybody to come with me,' murmured Miss Smith. 'It is better that I take dear Satan alone.'

The Duke looked astonished. 'But he isn't even saddled!'

'I never bother about saddles,' she laughed. 'When I ride, I need only one thing to guide me.'

'And what is that?'

'Love. Just love.'

She bowed, and stepped into the darkness. When she had gone, the Duchess took the Duke's arm and led him back to the study. 'Never in my life have I met such a sweet young thing,' she said. 'She hardly seems human.'

The Duke agreed. 'Hardly human,' he echoed.

If we had been walking with Miss Smith at that moment, through the darkness towards the stables, we might have agreed that she was hardly human. She was gliding rather than walking, skimming over the ground like a great big bat. When she reached Satan's stall and opened it and leapt on to his back, they seemed to join together as if they were one and the same creature, half horse and half witch. If they had swept by you in the country lanes, you would have felt a cold wind as they passed, and in the distance you would have seen a trail of crimson sparks.

Chapter Eight

Snowdrop woke with a start. A moment ago he had been far away, dreaming of a distant meadow where he could frisk away to his heart's content—a meadow which nobody would ever enter except the little mistress whom he had lost. In his dream he had seen her very clearly, walking towards him with a lump of sugar—lovely white sweet sugar which would not give him a pain.

As he blinked the sleep away he realized what had awoken him. It was Dumbelle, the mouse who was his sole companion. She was scratching away at the main beam overhead, and she was scratching faster than ever before—so fast, indeed, that when he looked up a lot of wood shavings fluttered down into his eye. However, he did not complain because he knew that she was his friend, and if only she had been able to speak he would not have felt so lonely. There were a lot of things he would have liked to ask her. For example, why did she spend so much time scratching away at that old beam? Was she going to make a nest? Whatever the reason, her small sharp teeth were certainly having a great effect on the beam, which was already nearly sawn in half. If she went on at this rate he was afraid that one day it might break in two and fall down on his head, and sometimes he wondered whether he ought to ask her to stop. But if he did she might go away, and he would be lonelier than ever.

Suddenly, Dumbelle stopped scratching, sat up on her

hind legs and stared through a hole in the woodwork. Her nose was twitching, her tail was swishing to and fro and she seemed to be in a state of great excitement. Then she jumped off the beam, scurried down the wall and swiftly shovelled the shavings into the corner, as though she were frightened that somebody might find them. After which she dived under the straw and vanished from sight.

A moment later, Snowdrop understood the reason for her strange behaviour. In the distance he heard a clatter of hoofs, and at the same time he felt the chill down his spine that always warned him when Miss Smith was drawing near. Then he heard the creaking of the gate into the backyard and the murmur of her voice. She had come home, and she was not alone.

He shuffled across and stared through a crack in the wall.

What Snowdrop saw made his blood run cold.

Miss Smith was walking into the yard, and something else was walking behind her. What was it? For a moment he could not see clearly; he could only see a dark shadow. Then they both stepped into the light of the moon and he saw that it was, in fact, a horse.

But what a horse! It was the most enormous horse, and he did not have to look at it twice to realize that it was not at all the sort of horse with whom he could ever make friends. Apart from its size, it had the most hideous expression on its face.

Miss Smith was patting it on the nose and running her hands through its coarse bushy mane.

'Do you love me?' she crooned. 'You beautiful wicked monster, do you love me?'

The horse lifted its head and gave a blood-curdling neigh. You and I would not have understood the meaning of that sound, but Snowdrop understood it, and Miss Smith did too. It meant that yes he loved her very much, and that he was only too willing to follow her in any plot she might be hatching.

Miss Smith put her fingers to her lips. 'Sssh . . . my darling, or you will wake the neighbours. I quite agree with you, but we must be careful. And now there is something I have to tell *you*. But first you must have your supper.'

She went to the pump and came back with a bucket of cool sparkling water. Then she got a bundle of clean, fresh oats and a tub of newly mixed bran. While Satan was eating and drinking Snowdrop watched him hungrily, because the witch never gave him enough to eat or drink—only just enough to keep him alive.

'And now,' said the witch, 'I will tell you my plan. You will stay with me and sleep in a beautiful stable and every night we will go riding together. When it is very dark—so dark that nobody can recognize us—and you may bite anything that we meet on the road.'

At this point Satan opened his mouth as though he were about to show his approval by one of his horrible neighs, but the witch shook her head. 'No, my angel,' she said, 'You must listen in silence. What I am telling you is very secret.'

'But that is only the beginning,' she continued. 'You and I, my lamb, are going to be very rich—so rich that we shall be able to ride round the whole world together doing just what we want. And the reason we are going to be so rich is because there is going to be a tremendous race, and because all these stupid humans are going to bet thousands and thousands of pounds on that race, and because *you* . . . my darling . . . are going to win it. Do you see? Ssh . . . not a sound! Just nod, if you understand.'

Satan nodded, keeping his wicked red eyes fixed upon her.

'Splendid!' For a moment she paused, lifting her green eyes to the moon. 'There are still a lot of details to be worked out,' she went on at length, 'but you can leave all that to me. You needn't worry your pretty little head about it. There is only one thing I have to ask you to do. And I am afraid that you won't like it at all. Until the race is run—you will have to behave yourself. You will have to pretend to be good.'

At the word 'good' Satan bared his teeth.

'Don't look at me like that, my dear,' she said. 'I only said *pretend* to be good. I should hate you to be *really* good. I want you to grow wickeder every day. But I want the humans to *think* that you are good, because then they will believe all that we tell them and we shall get much more of their money. Do you understand?'

An awful grin came over Satan's face. He understood.

'There's a clever boy', she murmured, stroking him on the forehead. 'Now show me how good you can look.'

For a moment Satan hesitated. He was so used to being bad, and looking bad too, that he had forgotten how to look anything else. But he made a great effort, and stopped lashing his tail, and pursed his mouth to conceal his dreadful teeth, and raised his eyes to the ceiling as though he were saying his prayers. And though he was still a very ugly horse, his appearance was not so alarming as it had been a moment before.

The witch was delighted.

'Wonderful! But don't overdo it, or you'll tire yourself out.'

Satan lowered his eyes and let himself look wicked again.

'There's one last thing,' said the witch, 'before you go to bed. I must tell you that I have another horse staying with me. His name is Snowdrop. He's only a pony and he won't get in your way, but I have to warn you of one thing about him. He is extremely *good*.'

Satan started to lash his tail.

'Yes, my dear, I know exactly how you're feeling because I feel just as strongly myself. All the same, you are *not* to bite him. It's no use grinding your teeth at me like that, my poppet. You are *not* to bite Snowdrop, or even kick him—at any rate, not yet, not until the race is over. After, of course, you can bite him and kick him to your heart's content. But in the meantime you have to pretend that you like him, because the humans absolutely love him. Snowdrop is the best advertisement we could possibly have. As long as we have him in our power, nobody will ever guess what we're plotting. Do you understand?'

Satan merely sniffed—a horrible sniff, which sounded like an escape of gas.

The witch shook her finger in his face. 'It's no use making those sweet little noises at me,' she said. 'You won't change my mind. I want to know if you understand.'

After a pause, Satan nodded his head. He understood.

'There's a clever boy,' she murmured. 'And now, my sweetheart, I shall show you the beautiful stable where you are going to sleep.'

She got up and beckoned to Satan, who lumbered to his feet and followed her across the yard. The moonlight shone brightly on them both, casting a greenish glow over the witch's hair and turning Satan's evil eyes into a strange shade of purple. A moment later, they had gone.

You may well imagine how Snowdrop felt after he had listened to this terrible conversation.

He had only one small grain of comfort. At least, Satan was not going to ill-treat him, provided that he obeyed Miss Smith's instructions. But *would* he obey them? Snowdrop had grave doubts about this. And even if

Satan behaved himself for the time being, the witch had told him that as soon as the race was over, he could bite and kick to his heart's content. It was all too awful to contemplate.

He went over to have a drink of water, but it was so dirty that he could not swallow it, and since there was nothing left to eat he lay down and tried to sleep. But as soon as he closed his eyes, he was roused by the sound of an angry buzzing. Looking up, he saw that he had a visitor, in the shape of Beelzebub. At the sight of him he shrank back under the cover of the straw, for he had already been stung several times by this frightening beetle, and he dreaded being stung again.

On and on buzzed Beelzebub, whirling round his head, like a sort of crazy helicopter. Deeper and deeper into the straw shrank Snowdrop, waiting for him to sting. But Beelzebub did not sting him, and gradually the buzzing grew less violent, and a different note crept into it. Evidently, the beetle was very angry with somebody, but it could not be with Snowdrop, because every time he came near the pony, he buzzed quite softly. It was only when he flew to the roof and looked through the crack that the buzzing became loud and fierce again. 'It is most extraordinary,' reflected Snowdrop, 'he seems to be angry with somebody outside, but who could it possibly be? There is nobody there but Miss Smith and Satan.' As soon as he thought of Satan, an idea occurred to him. Could it be Satan whom the beetle was buzzing about? Was he actually *jealous* of Satan? After all, he had good reason to be. Until today. Beelzebub had been the witch's special pet; he had gone everywhere with her, nestling in her hair. But she had not taken him with her when she went to the Duchess's, and when she returned she had brought back Satan, whom she obviously loved.

The more he thought about it, the more he was convinced that he was on the right track. If only he could ask Beelzebub outright! But it is a fact of nature that ponies and beetles have never been able to communicate with one another. Beelzebub could have gone on buzzing his head off for hours on end without Snowdrop understanding a single word he was trying to say.

All the same, there was a soothing sound about the buzzing, and when the beetle came to rest on his forehead, he did not flinch. Indeed, he quite liked the sensation, because Beelzebub began to stroke him, very gently, with his wings, as though he were trying to show him that they were friends.

'Well,' thought Snowdrop, 'a friend is a friend, even if it is only a beetle, and even if it has rather a bad reputation. And now I have *two* friends, because Dumbelle seems also to be on my side. So perhaps I should be grateful for small mercies.'

And with this comforting reflection, he sank into a dreamless sleep.

Chapter Nine

'*We are getting nowhere,*' exclaimed Mrs. Judy. '*Sometimes I* feel like washing my hands of the whole business.'

'Oh, Granny, you mustn't say that!' Judy looked at her with reproach. 'Think of poor Trotsky.'

Mrs. Judy glanced towards the turkey, who was strutting up and down by the hedge, with the ostrich feathers sprouting out of his behind.

'Why should we be so sorry for poor Trotsky?' she demanded. 'He's got quite used to those feathers. In fact he'd be furious if anybody tried to remove them.'

'Yes . . . but only because *you* persuaded him that he should be proud of them. That was one of the kindest things you ever did.'

'It wasn't kind at all,' snapped Mrs. Judy, who hated being paid compliments. 'It was the obvious thing to do. I couldn't have spent the rest of my life with a turkey who was always carrying on about his tail.'

Judy sighed. Her granny could sometimes be quite difficult. 'Well,' she said, 'even if we forget about Trotsky, we ought to remember Snowdrop.'

'I've never even seen Snowdrop.'

'No. But you could, if we went over to Meadowstream. We should be sure to see him, sooner or later, trotting up and down the street with the laundry wagon.'

Mrs. Judy snorted impatiently. 'And then what would we do? Stand in the middle of the road and stop him?

Take him out of harness and bring him here? Take Miss Smith off to the police station? Do try to be practical, my dear. If we did anything like that *we* should land up in the police station ourselves.'

Judy had to admit that her granny was talking common sense.

'Besides,' she continued, 'what have we got to go on? Where's the evidence against Miss Smith? Apart from the fact that she did those peculiar things to Trotsky—and even now, we can't be absolutely certain that she *was* responsible—what else is there? Precious little! I admit that it was strange that Snowdrop wouldn't touch your sugar, but then she *may* have been telling the truth when she told you that he'd been stealing from her kitchen. Then there are all those bats that Mrs. Greenapple saw sitting on the trees outside the laundry in the middle of the night. That's certainly bad, very bad indeed. But how do we know she *did* see them? She may have been making it all up. The one thing that really worries me is the green smoke coming out of Miss Smith's nose. Are you quite positive that you saw it? Would you swear to it in a court of law?'

'Yes, Granny, I would swear it on the Bible.'

The old lady sighed deeply. 'Then that settles it. As I told you before, the green smoke can mean only one thing. Miss . . . Smith . . . is . . . a . . . witch. So where do we go from there? Ought we to take the bull by the horns and go straight to the laundry? I think not. I doubt whether we'd find out very much, and we'd only arouse her suspicions.'

'Couldn't I go alone?' asked Judy eagerly. 'If I went in the middle of the night. I could creep in while she was asleep.'

'I wouldn't hear of it. It would be far too dangerous.

Have you forgotten that witches always sleep with one eye open? They should have taught you that at school. No witch *ever* closes both eyes at the same time. Even if she wanted to, she couldn't. Witches' eyes are quite different from yours or mine.'

'Well, I can't think of a better idea.'

'Maybe not. But I can.' The old lady sat up with a smile. 'We shall go to the Duchess's!'

'Why ever should we go *there*?'

'Frankly, my dear, I'm not sure. I suppose it's what you would call a "hunch". But ever since you told me about Miss Smith driving off in the Duchess's Rolls-Royce, I've been thinking how very strange it was. Duchesses do *not* go driving all over the place with their washerwomen. It's my belief that Miss Smith has cast a spell over her. And if she has . . .'

'Yes, Granny?'

'If she has, I shall know the signs. And then I shall know what to do!'

By now, Mrs. Judy was in a state of considerable excitement. She bustled around, patting her hair and straightening her blouse and giving Judy a great many urgent instructions. First she had to hurry off to the shed, to pump up the tyres of the tricycle. Then she had to climb up the tree to fetch down her one and only hat, and give it a good dusting. Finally, she had to run to the kitchen cupboard and take out a bottle of her celebrated dandelion wine.

'Do you think the Duchess will really like that?' asked Judy as the old lady dropped the bottle into her carpet-bag.

'Whether she likes it or not, she'll drink it,' snapped the old lady. 'And don't stand there asking such foolish questions. We've no time to lose.'

And before Judy could reply, she had jumped on to her tricycle and was pedalling away across the sunlit meadow.

Though she would never have admitted it, even Mrs. Judy felt rather overawed as they rode up the long drive that led to Meadowstream Castle. She had not realized that it was so huge and so grand, with so many lofty towers and battlements. The lawns were covered with statues of ladies with no clothes on, and in and out of the statues wandered hundreds of peacocks, who stared at them as they passed with very superior expressions.

Besides, she was feeling quite nervous about the plan which she invented for getting into the Castle. It had sounded simple when she had confided it to Judy, but now she was not so sure.

The idea was that she should call herself Mrs. Smith, and pretend that Miss Smith was her long-lost niece. If the witch really had cast a spell over the Duchess, she would be only too eager to meet anybody bearing the same name. But once they *had* met, what would she think? The witch, apparently, had turned herself into a very beautiful and stylish young woman, and nobody could call Mrs. Judy either beautiful or stylish, particularly when she was wearing such a peculiar hat. Supposing the Duchess were to call her an impostor and have her turned out of the house? However, it was no use meeting trouble half-way, and so, followed by Judy, she pedalled bravely up to the porch, mounted the steps and rang the bell.

It seemed hours before anybody answered it. Then they heard footsteps coming across the marble hall and the doors swung open to reveal a very tall young footman, wearing a uniform covered with gold braid.

'Yes, moddom?' he enquired, in the coldest of tones.

'We have come to see the Duchess,' said Mrs. Judy.

The footman raised his eyebrows. He was astonished that so common and shabby a creature as this old woman should dare to imagine that she would even be allowed to enter the Castle at all.

'Her Grace,' he observed 'is HOUT.' After which he began to close the door.

'One moment, my man!' retorted Mrs. Judy, who was not used to being addressed in this manner. 'I have reason to believe that her Grace is not out at all. I have also reason to believe that she is extremely anxious to see me.' She fixed him with an even haughtier stare than he was wearing himself. And then, to put him in his place once and for all, she hoisted her carpet-bag into his arms. 'I shall be obliged if you will carry this for me' she said icily. 'And you may announce us without delay.'

Staggering under the weight of the bag, the footman took a step backwards. His expression changed. He had an uneasy feeling that perhaps he had been wrong about this extraordinary old person. In spite of her shabby clothes, she spoke as though she were accustomed to being obeyed. She might even be a person of some importance. He would have to watch his step.

'Very well, moddom,' he said, swallowing his pride and placing the carpet-bag on the marble floor. 'If you would take a seat I will endeavour to find her Grace. May I have the name, if you please?'

'The name is Smith.'

This information had an immediate effect on the footman, whose behaviour suddenly became quite respectful. Ever since the witch had lunched at the Castle, her name had been constantly on the Duchess's lips . . . how wonderful she was, how beautiful and how clever. And it was not only the Duchess who had been so impressed, for the story of Miss Smith's visit to Satan had spread right through the staff. The stable-boys had told it to the grooms, who had told it to the gardeners, who had told it to the cooks and the footmen and the housemaids. They were all thrilled by Miss Smith because they were sure that she was going to make them a lot of money. They had always known that Satan was the fastest horse in the world, but until the arrival of the witch nobody had been able to ride him. Now all this was changed. When Satan entered the next big race, which would be quite soon, they were all going to back him. The footman himself had decided to put a whole month's wages on him.

That is why the name of Smith had such a magical effect on the footman. 'Thank you, moddom,' he murmured. He gave a low bow, hurried across the hall and ran up the marble staircase.

As soon as he had gone Mrs. Judy sat down and put her finger to her lips. 'So far, so good,' she whispered. 'Now listen carefully. Leave all the talking to me, do you understand? And whatever I say, try not to look surprised. I'm afraid I may have to say several things that are not quite—well, not exactly . . .'

'You mean you'll have to tell a lot of fibs?' interrupted Judy.

'I suppose you might put it like that.'

'Well, I think that's quite splendid,' said Judy calmly. 'After all, it's in a good cause.'

Mrs. Judy had no time to reply, because the Duchess was already hurrying down the stairs.

'Dear Mrs. Smith,' she exclaimed, holding out her hand, 'such a pleasuah!'

Mrs. Judy murmured that she hoped her visit was not inconvenient. At the same time she bent down and extracted the bottle of dandelion wine. 'I have brought you a little present.'

'For me? A present? How kind!' The Duchess took the bottle and regarded it rather doubtfully. 'What does one do with it? Does one drink it?'

'That is the idea.' As she spoke she took the cork out.

The Duchess thought this was a little unusual, and she could not understand why Mrs. Judy was wearing such an old-fashioned hat. However, the fact that her name was Mrs. Smith was quite enough to make her overlook such minor peculiarities, and so—after a delicate sniff—she took a small sip of the wine.

'Most refreshing,' she said, firmly putting back the cork. 'And now let us go and sit down in my little boudoir and you can tell me all the news.'

She led the way down a long gallery lined with portraits of the Duke's ancestors. As Judy looked up at them she thought that she had never seen such a lot of disagreeable old fuddy-duddies; most of the gentlemen were wearing suits of armour and most of the ladies were sitting on thrones with crowns on their heads. Not one of them was smiling.

The Duchess's 'little boudoir' was about the size of a tennis-lawn with a lofty painted ceiling and even more ancestors on the walls. She sank on to a sofa, placing the bottle on a table by her side, and motioned to them to sit beside her.

'You must forgive me for bringing you to my little boudoir,' she said, 'but I thought it would be cosier than sitting in one of the ballrooms. And now I want to hear all your news. You have come about the race, no doubt. Tell me, how is dear Satan?'

Mrs. Judy had not the faintest idea what she was talking about. You must remember that neither she nor Judy had yet heard about the race. Indeed, nobody knew about the race except Miss Smith and, of course, the people in the Castle, because the witch had impressed upon them that they must keep it a secret until Satan had won and made all their fortunes.

'Dear Satan,' echoed the old lady, wondering what was coming next. 'He is . . . yes . . . he is as well as can be expected. In fact, better.' At the same time she pushed the bottle of wine a little nearer to the Duchess's hand.

'Splendid!' exclaimed the Duchess. 'Such a marvellous horse!' Her eye lit on the bottle. 'Really this wine is quite delicious! Do you think I might have another tiny sip?'

'Please help yourself,' urged Mrs. Judy. The more tiny sips the Duchess had the better, because then she would be more likely to tell the truth.

She took a sip that was not at all tiny and set the bottle down again. 'Quite the most marvellous horse in the world. And all thanks to your charming young relation. By the way, you *are* related to Miss Smith?'

'Very closely,' fibbed Mrs. Judy.

'I thought so. Tell me more about her.'

Mrs. Judy hesitated. 'Well . . . ' she began. And then she stopped, searching for something to say.

'Yes?' prompted the Duchess.

Judy came to the rescue. 'Granny always says that Miss Smith is so beautiful. Don't you, Granny?'

Mrs. Judy gulped and nodded.

'She *is* beautiful,' agreed the Duchess, beaming on the little girl. 'Never have I seen such eyes. Or such eyelashes. They must be at least an inch long.'

'They're longer than that,' corrected Judy, who was beginning to enjoy herself. 'The last time we saw her, Granny actually measured them.'

While she was making this rather naughty remark, she avoided catching her grandmother's eye.

'Really?' exclaimed the Duchess. 'And how long were they?'

Judy, with a very innocent expression, looked up to their ceiling. 'I can't quite remember.' Then she turned round in her chair and faced Mrs. Judy. 'Do *you* remember how long Miss Smith's eyelashes were, Granny darling?'

This was an important moment in our story. Because, as you have already learned, Mrs. Judy was a very truthful old person. And though she had told Judy that she herself might be obliged to tell a few fibs, she had not been prepared for Judy to do so. However, what could she do? If she were to say that she had not measured them at all, the Duchess might be suspicious, which would be most awkward. 'In for a penny, in for a pound,' she thought. Whereupon she looked the Duchess straight in the eye and said . . .

'Her eyelashes were exactly one inch and threequarters.'

'You don't say so?' The Duchess was most impressed. 'They must be the longest eyelashes in the world. But then, of course, she is unique in so many ways. And so modest too. Did she tell you about her strange adventure with Satan?'

'She did mention it, but not in any detail.'

'How typical of her! She *never* puts herself forward. May I tell you myself?'

This was just what Mrs. Judy wanted. So she said that she would love to hear about it, and whispered to Judy that she must not interrupt.

And now the Duchess came out with the whole story. How she had gone to the village and visited the laundry, how she had brought Miss Smith back to luncheon, how she had taken her out to the stables to see Satan—'Such a wicked horse, my dear—it even tried to bite the Duke!' —and how, with a few soothing words, Miss Smith had completely captivated it and transformed it into a creature that was as gentle as a lamb.

The Duchess was so affected by her own story that when she had finished it there were tears in her eyes.

'But then of course,' she said to Mrs. Judy, 'you knew all this before.'

'Only the rough outline,' fibbed Mrs. Judy. 'But you make it sound so much more real.'

The Duchess smiled. 'Thank you. And I am sure you will agree with me that only a very *good* young person could have had such an effect on poor Satan.'

Mrs. Judy did not agree at all. In fact, she very much disagreed. Such a monster as Satan would have not cared tuppence what a good person said to him. But if a very *bad* person had come his way, he would have listened to her. However, she kept these thoughts to herself.

'It is all quite wonderful,' she said. 'And now, tell me, is Satan going to run in a race?'

'Oh yes! Didn't you know? How silly of me—I was forgetting—you couldn't have known, because Miss Smith asked us to keep it a secret.'

'Why?'

The Duchess gave a tinkling laugh. 'I can see that you don't know much about the racing world, Mrs. Smith. The reason it must be kept a secret is because Satan will certainly win the race, and if everybody knew that he was going to win, they would all back him, and then we would not make nearly so much money. So will you please promise not to tell anybody?'

'I promise not to tell a soul.'

'But that is no reason why you should not back him yourself. Indeed, you should do it at once, even if you only bet quite a small amount. Do you happen to have a hundred pounds on you at the moment?'

Since Mrs. Judy had never possessed as much as a hundred pounds in her life she had no difficulty in replying truthfully to this question.

'Such a pity, because you could have given it to me and I could have placed the bet for you. Never mind, you must do it as soon as you get home.'

At this moment the footman entered.

'Excuse me, your Grace. May I have a word with you?'

'Yes, James. What is it?'

'It's the laundry, your Grace,' said the footman.

'The laundry? What about the laundry?'

'It's come back, your Grace.'

'Well?' She tapped her foot impatiently. 'What else would you expect it to do?'

'Quite, your Grace. But it's come back in a very peculiar state.'

'Peculiar? What do you mean?'

'It's all black, your grace.'

'*Black*?' The Duchess drew herself up as though she had been insulted. 'How can it possibly be black?'

'It *is*, your Grace. Jet black—and there's something else, your Grace; there's a beetle.'

She stared at him haughtily. 'Have you been drinking, James?'

'No, your Grace.'

'Then will you kindly tell me what this beetle has got to do with my laundry?'

'That's what none of us can understand, your Grace. But it *has* got something to do with it.'

'Then why don't you squirt something on it and make it go away?'

'We have done, your Grace. But it won't go away. What's more, it has bitten the cook.'

The Duchess stifled a scream. 'Heavens! My house

seems to have turned into a lunatic asylum. Black laundry! Beetles! Whoever heard of such a thing?' She rose to her feet. 'Excuse me, Mrs. Smith, but I really must go and see what is happening.' She hurried out of the room, closely followed by the footman.

It seemed ages before the Duchess returned, though it was in fact only a few minutes. She was in a terrible state, sobbing and wringing her hands.

'All my beautiful sheets', she moaned. 'All my lovely towels and pillow-cases. All ruined!' She paced the room, looking quite distracted. She caught sight of the bottle of dandelion wine and lifted it to her lips. 'You really must excuse me, Mrs. Smith,' she gulped, 'but I feel quite faint. Nothing like this has ever happened in the Castle before.'

'Can you think of any explanation?' enquired Mrs. Judy.

The Duchess gave a slight hiccup. The dandelion wine had begun to go to her head. 'Whatever it may be, I am sure that it has nothing to do with Miss Smith. It must be that horrible beetle!'

'What was it like?' demanded the old lady. Her voice was very tense.

'It was like no beetle that I have ever seen before. And it has bitten the cook.'

'That is indeed unfortunate,' said Mrs. Judy. 'But what was it *like*? What was so different about it?'

The Duchess shuddered. 'Its wings were bright purple.' She shuddered again. 'But what does that matter? What matters is that it has turned my laundry black. And that it has bitten the cook. The most dreadful shting—dear me, I am so upset that I can hardly speak—the most dreadful sting on the end of her nose.'

She lay back on the sofa, closed her eyes and began to fan herself with great agitation. The old lady nodded to Judy. The time had come for them to leave. She had learned all that she wanted to know. And even if there had been any more questions to ask, the Duchess was evidently in no fit state to answer them.

She rose from her chair and held out her hand. 'We must not detain you any longer,' she said. 'I am so very sorry that this happened.'

The Duchess regarded her with bleary eyes. 'Must you go?' she murmured. 'Then you must let me send you home in the Rollsh-Roysh.'

'I would not dream of putting you to so much trouble.'

'No trouble at all.' She struggled to a sitting position and called to the footman. 'James! These ladies will drive home in the Rollsh-Roysh.'

Having given this order she sank back on the sofa and closed her eyes.

'Nothing to do Mish Shmith,' she repeated, as though speaking to herself. 'It was that beetle. And it shtang the cook. I dread to think what she will give us for shupper.'

Judy had never driven in a Rolls-Royce before, and she was so excited that for the time being she forgot to ask the meaning of all the weird things that had been happening. She bounced about on the cushions, marvelling at their softness, and pushed all sorts of knobs and pressed all sorts of buttons, to switch on the radio and open the windows and turn on the electric fans. All too soon they arrived at the entrance to the meadow, where the chauffeur took Mrs. Judy's tricycle and her own bicycle out of the boot, and drove away. During the journey Mrs. Judy had said not a word, but as soon as they were sitting under the tree she began to speak.

'Well, my dear,' she said, 'that was quite a day.'

'Did you get what you wanted, Granny?'

'More than I wanted. There's a great deal that I don't understand at all.' She stared ahead of her, lost in thought.

'But I'm sure of one thing. The secret of it all will be found in that beetle. Why did he turn the laundry black? Ordinary beetles simply don't do that sort of thing. Of course, if we could discover that he had any connection with Miss Smith, that would explain a lot of things. She might have taught him all sorts of terrible tricks. But as far as we know, he has nothing to do with her.'

Suddenly Judy sat up in excitement. 'But he *has* something to do with her, Granny!'

And then Judy told her about how she had seen Beelzebub fluttering into Miss Smith's parlour, and how he had sat by the window, and how the witch had shooed him away.

'Why didn't you tell me all this before?' demanded Mrs. Judy.

'I'm afraid I forgot. Besides, she said he wasn't a beetle at all. She said it was a butterfly.'

'What do *you* think he was?'

'I could have sworn he was a beetle. But she seemed so positive.'

'What colour was he?'

'He had dark purple wings and a bright red body.'

'That doesn't sound like a butterfly to me.'

'She even knew his name,' added Judy. 'She said he was a Kronkpot. A Greater Kronkpot.'

'Stuff and nonsense,' exclaimed the old lady. 'When I was your age I used to collect butterflies, and I certainly never heard of a Kronkpot. The whole thing seems very fishy. Can you think of anything else?'

'Just one thing. She said that word—Kronkpot—three times, and each time she said it she seemed to be speaking directly *to* the beetle. As though he understood her, and I believe he did, because on the third time he flew away.'

'That settles it. It *was* a beetle, and they *are* working

together. And in case you didn't know it, when you get dark purple and bright red next to each other it's a very bad sign. Which means that he must be a very bad beetle.'

'I suppose it does,' said Judy. 'But somehow I didn't feel that he was.'

'Never mind what you felt. All that matters is that in some way or other he's mixed up with the witch—and I'm convinced that she *is* a witch. But that only makes it more mysterious. If he is really working for her, why should she get him to turn the Duchess's laundry black? She's her best customer.'

'Do you think, Granny, that perhaps he was working on his own? Do you think they might have quarrelled, and that he was doing it as a sort of revenge?'

Mrs. Judy nodded. 'Now, that *is* an idea. If it were true, it would make our task much easier. We might be able to contact him, put him on the Translator and find out what this is all about.'

'What really interests me,' said Judy, 'is that horse they call Satan. If he's so sure to win the race . . .' Then she hesitated.

'Well?'

'Would you mind if I emptied my money box and made a bet on him?'

'Mind?' snorted the old lady. 'I should mind very much indeed. It would be like making money out of the Devil. Would you want to do that?'

'No, I suppose I wouldn't.'

'Besides, he mightn't win at all. By the way, when is the race?'

'They didn't say, but I think it's quite soon.'

'Then you must go to the village tomorrow and find out. It's sure to be in the local paper.'

'But even when we've found out, what can we *do*?'

'For the moment, we can only wait and see. But you mustn't be too impatient, my dear. We aren't standing still. We know a lot more today than we did yesterday.'

But there was one thing that the old lady did not know. If she had known it, she might not have felt quite so happy about the situation.

What Mrs. Judy did not know was that Miss Smith had actually seen them driving home in the Duchess's Rolls-Royce. It was only by pure chance that this had happened. The witch had suddenly felt that she would like some poisonous toadstools for supper, so she had wandered across the fields to gather them. They grew by a stagnant pond which she often visited in order to stock up with her favourite frog spawn. While she had been gathering them she had heard the sound of a car in the lane, and then, looking up, she had seen the Rolls driving by, with Judy and her granny in it, and she was so shocked and dismayed that she dropped all the toadstools into the pond, where they were gobbled up by the frogs, who croaked at her in mocking tones.

'This,' she thought,' is the worst thing that could possibly have happened. Just when everything was going so splendidly, it may spoil all my plans.'

She began to pace up and down, wondering what she ought to do, asking herself all sorts of questions. Why had those two odious human beings gone to see the Duchess? What could they have told her? What did they actually *know*? 'Nothing,' thought the witch, trying to console herself. And yet, could she be sure? When you are a witch, you are bound to have a guilty conscience. You live in a permanent state of fear in case your sins should find you out. Of course, if you are caught red-handed, you can always cast another spell, but casting spells is very tiring and even the most powerful witches have not got an unlimited supply of energy. And what with one thing and another, Miss Smith had been working overtime ever since she came to Meadowstream. Satan, in particular, had taken a great deal out of her. She loved him, but he was demanding and since he had to be taken out every night for a wild gallop across country she never seemed to get her proper sleep.

Once again she asked herself . . . what did they actually know? She began to count on her fingers.

1. There was the turkey. That wretched bird had started the whole trouble. If she had not made ostrich feathers come out of its hateful behind, and if it had not run away to Mrs. Judy's House Under the Tree, none of this would have happened.

2. There was the green smoke. She was sure that Judy had seen it coming out of her nostrils, and she had told her abominable grandmother about it, and she had a strong suspicion that Mrs. Judy was a nosey old horror who might know what it meant.

3. There was Beelzebub. There was no getting away from the fact that Judy had seen Beelzebub, and that she had recognized him to be a beetle. And in spite of being told that he was a butterfly, she had not been convinced.

4. Finally, Snowdrop. He might be her greatest danger. Why? She could not have told you. After all, she had him completely in her power, and he was a wonderful advertisement, trotting down the High Street, looking so gleaming white. And yet, she was afraid of him. He was good. He was utterly, impossibly, revoltingly G . . . O . . . O . . . D. It was enough to make a girl feel quite faint. The witch ground her teeth. Well, she thought, even if there's nothing else I can do, I can be beastly to Snowdrop, so beastly that he'll wish he'd never been born.

With this happy, witch-like reflection, Miss Smith felt

much better. And she set out for home with a smile on her scarlet lips.

When she entered the parlour, the telephone was ringing.

Miss Smith was not fond of telephones, for the simple reason that whenever a witch takes up the receiver—particularly if the person at the other end happens to be another witch—blue sparks come out of it. Quite a lot of bright blue stinging sparks. This is why witches so seldom ring each other up.

However, it was not another witch. It was the Duchess.

'Yes, your Grace?' she murmured. 'Can I help you?'

'The most terrible thing has happened,' replied the Duchess. 'All my laundry has come back black.'

The smile faded from the witch's face. 'Black? How is that possible?'

'That is what I am asking *you*, Miss Smith; what's more, there was this dreadful beetle.'

'Beetle, your Grace?' Miss Smith felt as though her world were tumbling in ruins about her. 'Which beetle?'

At this point, they were cut off. The witch replaced the receiver, waiting for the Duchess to call back. Her mind was in a whirl. It seemed all too clear that Beelzebub had been up to something. But why? Had she been neglecting him? But even if she had, surely he could not possibly have done anything as outrageous as this?

The telephone rang again.

'Are you there, Miss Smith? We were cut off.'

'Forgive me, your Grace,' stuttered the witch, 'but I simply don't know what to think.'

'None of us knows what to think,' resumed the Duchess, 'but please do not think that we are blaming *you*. I am sure that it has nothing to do with you. So is the Duke. Indeed, he did not want me to tell you about it, but I felt that you ought to know. And if you should see that terrible beetle you must destroy it at once.'

'I will indeed.'

'Now, let us speak of happier things. How is dear Satan?'

The witch told her that dear Satan had never been better.

'And your sweet little pony? As fat and white as ever? Splendid!'

For several minutes the Duchess babbled on while the witch stayed there, grinding her teeth and stamping her feet. Finally she rang off.

As soon as she had replaced the receiver Miss Smith ran to the window and shouted, 'Pockle-poop!' You may remember that in Beetle Language this means, 'Come here!'

But Beelzebub did not appear. There was no sign of him at all.

'Pockle-poop this instant!' screamed the witch. 'If you don't pockle-poop, I shall, I shall . . .' She was choking with such anger that she could not finish the sentence.

Then an awful smile curled her lips. She might not be able to get hold of Beelzebub, but there was another creature on whom she could vent her rage . . . Snowdrop. She would go out to the stable this very instant and beat him within an inch of his life. He was the cause of all the trouble, she was convinced. And even if he weren't, she didn't care. She seized a riding crop and strode across the yard.

When the witch flung open the stable door, and when Snowdrop saw her standing there with the whip, he thought that his last hour had come. He began to tremble violently and shuffled over to the corner, waiting for the blows to fall. Out of sheer terror, he shut his eyes.

But nothing happened. For the witch had suddenly remembered that the Duchess had asked her, 'How is your *sweet* little pony?' Which meant, of course, that she had taken a fancy to Snowdrop and would keep an eye on him, and if she suspected that he was being ill-treated heaven knows what would come of it. And though Miss Smith did not care tuppence about heaven she cared very much indeed about the Duchess, who was the last person she could possibly afford to offend.

She let out a howl of rage and the whip fell from her hands. 'You snivelling little monster,' she yelled, 'you filthy white bundle of beastliness, just you wait till I get my hands on you! And don't you think that you haven't got it coming to you! As soon as Satan has won the race, I shall come home and thrash you within an inch of your life!'

She picked up the whip, and with a final snarl of rage, she slammed the door and locked it. Snowdrop hung his head and tears began to run down his cheeks.

But though he was still trembling, he had one grain of comfort—no, two grains of comfort. He was no longer quite alone. During the whole of this violent scene, if Miss Smith had only looked up to the stable ceiling, she would have discovered that she was being watched by two small pairs of eyes—the pale blue eyes of Dumbelle and the bright green eyes of Beelzebub. And both those pairs of eyes were lit by such a fierce fire of hatred that if looks could have killed, the witch would have dropped dead on the spot.

But alas, as we shall soon discover, she was still very much alive.

Chapter Ten

'Read it out to me, my dear,' said Mrs. Judy. 'My eyes are not as strong as they used to be.'

Judy had just come back from the village where she had gone to buy a copy of the local newspaper, and they were sitting under the tree in the cool of the evening having tea.

Judy smoothed out the paper on her lap, and read as follows . . .

MEADOWSTREAM RACES
SATURDAY JULY FIRST

'Heavens!' exclaimed the old lady. 'Only three weeks ahead!

Judy continued:

'The Races will be held in the Park of Meadowstream Castle, by kind permission of Her Grace the Duchess of Meadowstream.'

'Kind?' sniffed Mrs. Judy. 'What's kind about it? All she's thinking about is the money she's going to make. What else?'

'There's rather a lot,' replied Judy, glancing down the page. 'About the price of the tickets and that sort of thing. No . . . wait a minute . . . listen to this!'

THE OWNER OF THE WINNING
HORSE WILL RECEIVE
A SOLID GOLD CUP
PRESENTED BY
MISS SMITH

'*What*?' Mrs. Judy looked quite fierce. 'Solid gold presented by Miss Smith? Of all the insolence! How does a washerwoman get hold of a SOLID GOLD CUP?'

'Well, she's rather an unusual sort of washerwoman.'

'I should say she is, returning everybody's laundry black! *I* wouldn't give her a solid gold cup. I'd give her an enamel mug with a hole in the bottom. Get on with the advertisement.'

'There's not much else, except the names of the horses.'

'But that's the most important part of all, you silly girl. Read them out.'

Judy, with a sigh, read through the names. The names meant nothing to Judy—they were names like 'Lucky Charm' and 'Mary Jane' and 'Danny Boy'. But when she came to the last her voice trembled.

'Granny, guess the last name.'

'Satan? Just as I thought! And is it in very small letters?' Judy nodded.

'It would be. And the reason it's in very small letters is because neither the witch, nor the Duchess, nor any of them, want people to think that Satan will win. So that when they back him they will all make their fortunes. What are the odds?'

Judy bent over the newspaper. 'I don't really understand these things,' she faltered. 'But there's the number one thousand and then there's the number one.'

'I knew it! That means that if you were to put a pound on Satan and if he were to win, you would get a thousand pounds.'

Judy stared open-mouthed at her grandmother. 'But, Granny, I have over a pound in my money-box. And if I could win a thousand pounds . . .'

'What would you do with it?'

She thought for a moment. 'The first thing I would do would be to buy you a new carpet for your bedroom.'

'Which is very sweet of you, my dear. But you wouldn't be able to do it because Satan is NOT going to win that race.' She rose to her feet. 'Not over my dead body!' Even as she spoke, she uttered a scream, and put her hands to her head. Judy started up in alarm. 'Granny, Granny!' she cried. 'There's something in your hair!'

There was indeed. It was Beelzebub.

You may remember that the last time we met Beelzebub he was sitting up among the rafters of the stable, next to Dumbelle the mouse, glaring down at Miss Smith with hatred in his eyes.

There was more than one reason for this hatred. Satan was the first reason; he had begun it all. Until the arrival of this horse, Beelzebub had been the only one whom the witch loved. Not that she really *loved* him, because she was incapable of loving anything or anybody. All the same, she had at least looked after him, paying him a great deal of attention, and letting him have things his own way. Now all this was changed. She was so besotted by Satan that she hardly went near Beelzebub, and stopped giving him special titbits for dinner. Worst of all, she never took him on her midnight rides when she galloped with Satan over the moonlit fields. He would have loved to go on those rides, nestling in her hair. But she made him stay at home, and on the only occasion when he had fluttered out to join them, she had taken him back indoors and shut him up in a cupboard.

The other reason why he had turned against Miss Smith was more important. As he grew older he was beginning to understand two things. First, that the witch was a much more wicked person than he had ever realized. Second, that he himself was a much *less* wicked person than he had been brought up to believe. You must remember his history. When the witch had first seen him on the tombstone—a small, frightened ladybird who had lost his way —he had known nothing of the world and had no idea how to tell right from wrong. When she gave him a home and taught him her evil tricks, he took it all quite naturally, because he thought that this must be the proper way to behave. Quite frankly, he enjoyed some of the jobs he was given to do, particularly if they gave him an opportunity to spotty-spittle. He loved spotty-spittling and—as we know—became highly expert at it.

But he had not been *born* to spotty-spittle for the simple reason that he had not been born a beetle; he had been born a ladybird, and ladybirds are not beastly by nature. Perhaps the best proof that Beelzebub was not really wicked was the fact that although Miss Smith had tried to change his wings to black she had not been able to do so. All she could do was to change them to purple.

He was still a ladybird at heart, and now at long last, he knew it.

Which is why, on the day after Miss Smith had made that terrible scene in the stable, threatening to beat Snowdrop within an inch of his life, Beelzebub made his great decision. He had already tried to teach the witch a lesson by spotty-spittling on the Duchess's laundry. But that was no longer enough. He would have to leave Miss Smith altogether, and go over to the ranks of the enemy. For among the witch's enemies, he was now convinced, he would find his real friends.

'Granny!' Judy had cried. 'There's something in your hair! My goodness, I believe it's that beetle I saw at Miss Smith's!'

'Whatever it may be,' replied the old lady calmly, 'it's tickling. And though I may have bats in the belfry, I have not yet grown used to having beetles in the hair.' She was pleased with her little joke, and stood there chuckling to herself.

Judy held out her hand with the palm upwards. 'Beetle dear,' she said gently, 'please be a good boy and come out of Granny's hair.'

All at once Beelzebub—who had been buzzing away like mad—became quite silent. It was that word 'dear' that had done it. Nobody had ever called him 'dear' before. Slowly he crawled out of the old lady's hair and jumped on to Judy's hand.

'It *is* a beetle, Granny.'

As soon as Beelzebub heard her saying this he began to buzz again.

'Well, he doesn't seem to like being told so,' retorted Mrs. Judy. 'That's a very nasty sort of buzz.' She bent down and examined him more closely. 'What's more, he doesn't look like any beetle I've ever seen before. We must put him on the Translator at once.'

Judy sighed and hesitated. She had a rather poor opinion of the Translator. Nevertheless she fetched the pink satin cushion and gently sat Beelzebub down on it in front of the machine, while Mrs. Judy adjusted the trumpet and wound up the motor.

Wondering what they were going to do to him, Beelzebub began to buzz again. He was feeling rather frightened.

'Splendid!' exclaimed Mrs. Judy. 'Go on buzzing, my dear.'

But again, as soon as he heard the word 'dear,' Beelzebub became silent, and sat their blinking into the trumpet with a look of great contentment.

'What a nuisance! He's stopped. Never mind, he must have said something, even if it wasn't very much. Let's see what we've got.'

She pulled a lever, and a piece of paper fluttered out. Judy picked it up. 'There are only two words on it,' she said. 'The first is "lady".'

Mrs. Judy frowned. 'That's not much help. Do you think he means the Duchess? What's the other word?'

'Bird.'

'That's no good either. The only bird mixed up in this business is Trotsky, and we know quite enough about him already.' For a moment she stayed there, thinking. Then her old face wreathed with smiles. 'But of course!' she cried. 'How silly we are! He didn't give us two words . . . only *one* word "Ladybird".'

'Ladybird?' echoed Judy. Then she understood. 'Oh, Granny, you *are* clever! Does it mean that he's trying to tell us that he isn't a beetle at all?'

'What else could it mean? Listen to him!' Beelzebub was now buzzing very loudly. 'There's nothing angry about that buzz. He's delighted. In a minute, we'll put him on the Translator again, but first I want to make a little experiment.'

She went to the cupboard, and brought a bottle covered with cobwebs. 'I don't have to be told, my dear, that you think me very old-fashioned, and that you don't believe in magic . . .'

'I do believe in magic,' protested Judy.

'I mean, *my* sort of magic. Most of the magic you've

seen, so far, has been black magic—the sort that's used by that awful Miss Smith. The reason you've seen so little of my sort of magic—apart from the Translator—is because at my age magic is very tiring. When I was young, people came to me from all over the world. Now that I've retired, they don't come any more. I don't want them to. But I've still a few tricks up my sleeve, and one of them is contained in this bottle of H two O. And you know what that stands for.'

'It stands for water.' Judy knew the answer to that question because she was learning chemistry at school.

'So it does. Water—Truth Water, in this case.'

She dusted the cobwebs from the bottle and held it up to the light. 'Yes, it seems all right.' She took out the cork and sniffed. 'Still quite sweet, even after all these years.'

'But what does it *do*, Granny?'

'It makes people tell the truth. If you put a single drop of this water on the tongue of anybody who's telling lies it makes the tongue go quite stiff and he can't speak. At this moment it is important that Beelzebub should tell the truth, even if he doesn't want to.'

She stepped softly over to Beelzebub, holding out the bottle. He sat there watching her. He was still frightened, but he stayed quite still. He knew that he was among friends.

Drop by drop the water sparkled from the bottle.

And now, when he felt the Truth Water dropping on to his wings, Beelzebub had the most extraordinary sensation. He felt as though he were drifting into the past, over the hills and far away—as though he were being washed clean again, with all his sorrows forgotten and all his sins forgiven. He felt a greater happiness than he had known since the beginning of his little life, when he had flown through the flowers in sunlit gardens. He was so happy that for a moment he thought that he must be dreaming—the most beautiful dream that any ladybird can ever have dreamt.

Then he heard Mrs. Judy's voice, and though he could not understand all she said, he knew that she was speaking words of happiness.

'His wings are growing lighter!' The old lady spoke in an excited whisper. 'That horrible purple is going away and . . . yes . . . he's turning red again. Look, my dear, look!'

Judy bent down and looked, and indeed it was true. The purple was fading, and as it faded, the red began to appear—the most beautiful, joyful, glistening red—as red as the berries of Christmas holly. In less than three minutes he was red all over.

'He's beautiful!' cried Judy. 'But isn't he rather big for a ladybird?'

'We could probably make him smaller, later on, if that's what he wants. For the time being I think we should leave him as he is.' Mrs. Judy spoke to him directly. 'Don't you think that would be best, dear?'

There it was again, that beautiful word 'dear'. When he heard it Beelzebub begun to buzz again, very softly—more like a purr than a buzz. He was a very happy ladybird. Maybe the happiest ladybird in the wide, wide world.

Chapter Eleven

While these things were happening, there was somebody else who was going even redder than Beelzebub, and that 'somebody' was Miss Smith.

In the whole of her career she had never been so enraged. She felt like bursting. For one thing, she had lost a lot of money. She would have to replace the Duchess's laundry and she dreaded to think how much that would cost. But far more serious was the disappearance of Beelzebub, and the fact that he had probably gone over to the enemy. The more she thought about it, the more convinced she was that he had flown off to that ghastly old woman under the tree.

There was one thing she must do without a moment's delay. She must find out how much Mrs. Judy actually *knew*.

She hurried over to the telephone, and dialled the number WIT 0734. There is not a number that you will find in the book because the letters WIT stand for the Witches Exchange, which is not connected with our own telephone system. In case you feel tempted to dial a number starting with WIT you are strongly advised not to do so, for you might get an electric shock. As we mentioned before, when you ring up a witch blue sparks come out of the machine.

So it was on this occasion. As soon as Miss Smith had lifted the receiver, a whole stream of blue sparks shot out, and she felt as if she were being stung by hundreds of very sharp wasps.

The lady whom she was ringing up was another witch called Miss Jones. She was a mere girl compared with Miss Smith, indeed, she had only just celebrated her hundred and fiftieth birthday. However she was well thought of in the witches' world, and had built up a good position for herself.

The telephone buzzed away and then Miss Smith heard a voice at the end of the line. It sounded rather cross.

'Hullo? Hullo? Who is it?'

'This is Miss Smith.'

'I can't hear you. The sparks are very bad today.'

'Miss Smith,' repeated the witch at the top of her voice. 'And the sparks are just as bad at my end as at yours. Hold on for a minute and they'll die down.' A few moments later, the sparks stopped. 'That's better. Can you hear me now?'

'Oh, it's *you*,' exclaimed Miss Jones. 'How lovely of you to ring me up! I trust you are keeping well?'

'Very well, thank you,' replied Miss Smith, grinding her heel on to the last of the blue sparks, which was beginning to burn a hole in the carpet.

'Splendid! And what can I do for you?'

'Well, there is just one little favour. Do you happen to have a copy of the "Witches' Who's Who"?'

'Of course. I never go anywhere without it.'

'Then would you be so very kind as to look somebody up for me? The name is Judy. Mrs. Judy.'

'I've never heard of her.'

'No, you wouldn't have done. She isn't One of Us. She's good.'

'How horrible! But how could such a person get into the "Witches' Who's Who"? Surely they don't include such creatures?'

Miss Smith tapped her foot impatiently. 'I must remind you, my dear, that at the end of the book there is a whole chapter on Good People. Printed in jet black.'

'So there is! If you'll hold on, I'll get the book and look her up.'

A few moments later Miss Jones was back on the line.

'This Mrs. Judy of yours *is* in the book,' she said. 'She sounds quite frightful. I hope you're not mixed up with her in any way?'

'Never mind what I'm mixed up with,' retorted Miss Smith. 'Just read out what it says.'

In tones of great disgust, Miss Jones read as follows:

' "Mrs. Judy. Born 1895 and married an extremely good clergyman. Had a daughter who married an even better clergyman. After many years of happy marriage both clergymen are dead and almost certainly in heaven." '

Here Miss Jones paused. 'Did you ever hear of such ghastly goings on?' she breathed.

'Quite,' agreed Miss Smith. 'It is enough to make one feel quite sick. But do get to the point. . . . What does this old horror *do*? What has she actually *invented*?'

'Wait a minute! Ah—here we are! Mrs. Judy seems to have invented two things that might be very dangerous. Listen: "Among Mrs. Judy's inventions is a preparation called Truth Water which—she claims—compels people and animals to tell the truth." '

'Disgusting,' snorted Miss Smith. 'Go on.'

Miss Jones continued . . . ' "However, Mrs. Judy's most remarkable invention is called the Translator, a machine which, so she claims, actually translates the sounds of animals, birds and even insects into human speech. We have not been able to check this claim, because Mrs. Judy has guarded her secret very jealously, and refuses to disclose any of the details. However, we have reason to believe that there is some truth in it. If so, all witches are advised to steer clear of this dangerous person." '

'I knew it!' cried Miss Smith. 'I knew it from the first moment I set eyes on her.'

'But what has she got to do with *you*, dear?' enquired Miss Jones. 'You never have anything to do with animals. In fact, you hate them as much as I do.'

'More,' snapped Miss Smith. 'Much more. But at this moment I happen to have a great deal to do with animals, particularly a horse called Satan, who is going to win me thousands and thousands of pounds by winning a race.'

There was a moment's pause. Then Miss Jones spoke again, in the sweetest of tones. 'Darling,' she said, 'you know I never bet or go to horse races. It's against my principles. All the same, if you are really sure that Satan is going to win, I wonder if you'd be an angel and put a little something on him for me?'

Miss Smith could have slapped herself for telling Miss Jones about Satan. Because if everybody began to back him, the odds would go down, and she would not make nearly so much money.

For a moment she was too angry to speak. Then she forced herself to snap, 'How much?'

'Oh, just a trifle. Shall we say . . . ten thousand pounds?'

Miss Smith's face, as she answered this question, was not at all pretty. It looked like the face of a very ill-natured vulture on the point of biting the nose off its dearest friend. But she managed to conceal her feelings.

'Of course, darling. How much did you say? Ten thousand? You're sure you wouldn't like to put on a little more?'

'No, thank you, dear. It's all I happen to have in my bag at the moment.'

'I'll put it on for you tomorrow,' said Miss Smith.

Whereupon the two ladies rang off. As they did so, both their receivers sent out showers of blue sparks and for the next five minutes they were kept very busy stamping them out of the carpet.

We must now switch the clock forward till midnight. If you are reading this book at bed-time you should put it aside until tomorrow morning, because exciting things are going to happen, which might give you nightmares.

But first we must tell you about the events of the afternoon.

When the witch had finished telephoning, she was so angry that she seized the riding-crop from the wall, rushed across the yard, flung open the stable door and slashed Snowdrop very hard, three times, across the back. After that she took away his dinner and gave a savage kick to his water-bucket, so that all the water ran down the drain. When she slammed the door again she left the wretched pony stinging with pain, and so hungry and thirsty that he felt he was going to faint.

And yet, if you had seen him trotting down the High Street two hours later while the witch went about her errands, you would have said that there could not be a happier pony in the world. How could this happen? How could this half-starved, ill-treated little creature be so quickly transformed into such a splendid animal?

Well—the bruises are easy to account for, because the witch had thrown a white cloth over his back so that nobody could see them.

But how had he suddenly become so plump, when he had not had a proper meal for weeks?

The explanation of Snowdrop's apparent plumpness

and sleekness is sad to relate. It lay in the cleverest and wickedest of all Miss Smith's inventions, which was called the Puffer.

The Puffer was a round white pill about the size of a pea, which looked quite harmless, like most of the pills which you see in the chemist's. Indeed, it was actually in a London chemist's that she had first got the idea for it. She had walked in one afternoon to buy a few deadly poisons, and while she had been wandering around she had noticed that although there were a great many pills for making humans thin, there seemed to be none for making them fat—at least, not *really* fat. It occurred to her that if she could invent such a pill it might come in quite handy on all sorts of occasions. For instance, there were times when she had to disguise herself as a hospital nurse, in order to be able to cast spells over the relatives of some of her richer clients. In the past, she had contented herself by bringing her victims out in warts, but if she could also make them enormously fat, this would be even more satisfactory, and might give her an excuse for charging higher fees.

So she bought one of the bottles of pills for making people thin, and took it home, and for the next week she sat up every night, trying out various ways by which the thinning pills could be made to work in reverse, and have the opposite effect. You would have been quite alarmed if you could have seen her making these experiments. She worked in near darkness, bending over bowls and testtubes, which hissed and bubbled, casting greenish shadows on to the ceiling. You would have been especially alarmed if you had been present when her efforts were crowned with success. For when the witch felt that she had at last made the right sort of pill, she decided to take one herself. And as soon as she had swallowed it she began to swell out, and she went on swelling and swelling till she looked like a monstrous balloon. She became so swollen that she could hardly breathe and she was terrified in case she was going to explode. But gradually the swelling stopped, and after a few hours she was her normal skinny self again.

That was the origin of the Puffer. Even to this day it is used by witches all over the world, under the name of Miss Smith's Patent Puffers. She still makes quite a nice little income from it.

And that is the reason why Snowdrop always looked so sleek and fat.

However, we were going to switch the clock forward to midnight and now the time has come to do so.

When Snowdrop was shut up in his stable again after making the rounds of the village, he lay down with only one idea in his head. He wanted to die. He saw nothing ahead of him but pain and hunger and loneliness, and he wanted to get away from it all, for ever.

But he could not die, because he knew that the witch would keep him alive as long as he was of any use to her. He could not even sleep. However tightly he closed his eyes, he remained wide awake, shivering, with his ears cocked, listening to every sound from the outside world.

Then, as the shadows began to fall, he became aware that something strange was happening overhead. The great beam that supported the ceiling seemed to be slowly altering its shape. As he looked up he saw, with a start of alarm, that it was actually beginning to bend in the middle. He got up on his feet and shuffled over to the corner, in case it should fall on top of him. As he did so he saw Dumbelle run along it and take a flying leap on to the floor, where she stayed looking up at the beam, her tail frisking backwards and forwards, in a state of great excitement.

What did it all mean? For several days he had been so

miserable that he had forgotten all about the little mouse. Although he was grateful for her presence, she was not much of a companion, because they did not speak each others' language. However, at least he knew that she was his friend, and he guessed that if she was so excited, it must be because she was working for him.

He went on staring up at the beam, with Dumbelle sitting on the floor beside him, frisking her tail, and suddenly he realized what was happening. Dumbelle was planning his escape! If the beam broke in two it would bring down the whole roof and at least two of the walls and he would be able to jump to freedom.

His heart began to beat so fast that he felt as though he had been running a race.

But supposing the beam were to break too soon, while the witch was still at home?

His heart beat faster and faster, and Dumbelle's tail whisked even more swiftly backwards and forwards. In silence they waited while the hours ticked slowly by. From time to time a creaking sound came from the beam, as though it were about to break, but it still held in place, though only by a few thin shreds. Now and again there would be a flutter of sawdust, and another creak, and one of the walls was beginning to sag. The moon rose higher in the heavens, and from the neighbouring woods came the shrill squeak of the bats gathering in the branches, as they always did, to pay their nightly homage to the witch.

But still the beam held.

It must have been nearly midnight when the sound of the witch's footsteps was heard in the yard telling them that she was going off on one of her midnight rides with Satan. A few moments later came the clatter of Satan's hooves, striking sparks on the cobblestones. As they rode past there came the familiar chill, as though an icy wind was blowing.

The sound of the hoofs echoed away into the distance. There was complete silence.

And now Dumbelle went into action.

With a few lightning leaps she scaled the wall, dashed out on to the beam, and began gnawing as she had never gnawed before. Her tiny teeth sank into the wood, tearing it away in swift sharp shreds and suddenly there was a great grinding and groaning and splintering. The beam split in two and crashed to the floor; the walls crumbled and collapsed, making a great clutter as they fell into the yard. From the woods came the hideous clamour of the bats, wheeling around in the night sky, squeaking in anger and alarm. Into the dirty stable streamed the clean white moonlight.

Snowdrop lifted his head and gave a long sweet neigh of happiness. At last, he was free.

But Snowdrop's feeling of happiness was short-lived. He might be free, but what was he to do with his freedom? Where was he to go?

For the moment he could not answer these questions. Meanwhile, there was not a moment to be lost. In spite of the lateness of the hour, some of the neighbours might be awake, and come rushing round to see what all the uproar was about. And if they found him they would tie him up again, and hand him back to the witch.

Softly he began to step through the rubble. But just as he was about to put his foot over the fallen wall, he heard a squeak. Looking down he saw that it was Dumbelle, gazing up at him with her bright pink eyes.

'Squeak!' said Dumbelle again. 'Squeak!' And then, a very long . . . 'Squee . . . squee . . . squeak!'

Snowdrop could hardly believe his ears. In all the time

that he had known Dumbelle he had never heard even a whisper come out of her funny little mouth. Could it mean that she was going to be able to speak again, and that he would be able to understand her? This was another question which would have to wait till later on.

At least he understood the meaning of that 'squeak'. She was trying to tell him that she wanted to be taken with him. As this thought occurred to him, he felt ashamed of himself. How could he have forgotten his little friend? Very gently he bent down and gave her a lick with his tongue. Though he was not a very big pony, she happened to be a ridiculously small mouse, so that the lick knocked her flat on her back. But within seconds she was up again, and scrambling into his mane.

And now at last they could go.

Softly he stepped into the yard, and then out into the road, where he paused, looking from right to left. So far, so good. The lights of the neighbouring houses were out, and all the bats had flown. Softly, softly down the street, towards the bridge that spanned the river. Then, just as he was about to trot over it, he heard a sound in the distance. His ears went back and he stopped dead in his tracks. The sound came closer and suddenly he knew what it was—the sound of Satan's hooves, galloping at top speed towards him.

Without a second's hesitation he took a flying leap over the bridge, straight into the river. It was deep and swiftly running, but he landed on his feet, with his neck above water. A few seconds later, Satan whirled past with the witch astride him. There was a flurry of sparks and then they were gone.

He stayed quite still in the icy water, trying to work things out. Why had the witch come back? Where had she gone to look for him? Where could he run for safety?

But he was so weak, that he could not think clearly. All he knew was that if he did not get out of the river he would be swept away and drowned. He plunged forward, stumbled and nearly went under, and then, with a final effort scrambled up the bank, where he staggered on to the grass. As he lay down he heard a tiny squeak from above, telling him that Dumbelle was still safely settled in his mane.

But he could not stay here. The witch might return at any moment and she would see his white coat and that would be the end. With another effort he got on to his feet. There were some woods in the distance and perhaps he could shelter in their shadow, where his whiteness would be less visible. He began to trot towards them. But he could only go very slowly and shakily and he could no longer see clearly. What's more, the clouds had swept over the moon, so that he kept falling over. Soon he had lost all sense of direction and was ambling round in circles. How long his brave little heart kept him going we shall never know, but the moment came when he could go no longer. With the last of his remaining energy he leapt a hedge, and crashed into a ditch by the side of the road.

And it was there that Judy found him a few hours later, lying quite still in the morning sunlight.

Chapter Twelve

Judy had gone out to pick mushrooms after breakfast, and it was only by chance that she had taken this road. Indeed, she was just about to turn off it, because she noticed that it led to Meadowstream Castle, and she had no wish to meet the Duchess at this hour, particularly when she was so shabbily dressed.

Then she saw Snowdrop lying in the ditch.

For a moment she thought that he was dead, and she stopped in the middle of the road, feeling as though she would like to run away. Then she noticed that he was still breathing faintly and she tiptoed towards him. When she saw his terrible condition her heart leapt with pity. He was so thin that his ribs were sticking out; there were great big bruises on his back and his coat was specked with blood from the thorns and the brambles.

'Oh, you poor darling!' she cried. 'What have they been doing to you?'

Snowdrop woke from his dreams, shaking with terror at the sound of a human voice. But when he saw Judy and when she spoke again, he felt a sudden comfort. He knew that here was somebody who would do him no harm, somebody who wished him well, and this knowledge gave him the strength to rise to his feet.

When she saw him standing up, Judy's pity grew even greater.

'You poor, poor darling,' she cried again. 'You look

quite dreadful.' She put out her hand and gently stroked his mane. 'But never mind. It's going to be all right. I'm going to take you home.'

Snowdrop was surer than ever that he had found a friend. He lifted his head and gave a pathetic little neigh.

'That's better, my dear,' went on Judy. 'You're coming home with me. I know you want to rest, but it's not far, and we'll go slowly.'

She stepped back to examine him, wondering if he might be lame. As she did so, a curious thought crossed her mind. Hadn't she seen this pony somewhere before? Wasn't there something faintly familiar about him? But how could there be? The only pony she knew of was Snowdrop, who belonged to Miss Smith. And though she detested the witch, she had to admit that as far as Snowdrop was concerned, she certainly seemed to look after him very well. Why—she had seen him only yesterday, trotting down the High Street, looking very sleek and plump. Whereas this pony had obviously not had a decent meal for weeks.

And yet, there *was* something about him that reminded her of Snowdrop. It was all very mysterious.

'Never mind,' she said to him. 'It's of no consequence, really. All that matters, my dear, is that you're coming home with *me*. And whoever you belonged to before is never going to have you again. Never, never, never.'

And now, even as she spoke, things began to happen. Round the corner swept the Duchess's Rolls Royce.

The Duchess was sitting in the car by the side of a gentleman whose name was Lord Goldbags. When she saw Judy walking towards them, followed by Snowdrop, her first instinct was to tell the chauffeur to drive on. Never had she seen such a sight, like a pair of tramps. Then she thought better of it, because in spite of her silliness, she had quite a kind heart. Besides Judy, so she believed, was connected with her beloved Miss Smith, who could do no wrong. She told the chauffeur to stop.

'Good morning, my dear,' she said as the car drew to a halt. 'This is Lord Goldbags.'

Judy dropped a curtsey.

The Duchess's eyes fell on Snowdrop, and she gave a little scream. 'Wherever did you find that extraordinary creature?'

Judy had to do some rapid thinking. Whatever might happen, she was determined that nobody was going to take Snowdrop away from her. He was *here*, and she would go to any lengths to keep him, even if she had to lie about it, as now she did.

'I—I—b . . . b . . . bought him,' she stammered, 'at a fair.'

'But *why*? I've never seen such a poor, miserable object. He looks half-starved.'

Judy nodded. 'That's why I bought him. I was sorry for him.'

The Duchess smiled, and turned to Lord Goldbags. 'Isn't that sweet?' she purred. 'I forgot to tell you that this little girl is related to our beautiful Miss Smith, whom you met the other day.'

'Indeed?' replied his Lordship, looking at Judy with a new interest. 'The charming young lady who is training Satan?'

'The very same.'

Lord Goldbags beamed at Judy. 'You are a lucky little girl to have such a delightful relation,' he assured her. He spoke from the heart, for two reasons. He had been greatly fascinated by the witch. And he put a lot of money on Satan to win the race.

Judy dropped another curtsey.

The Duchess was just about to tell the chauffeur to go on, when she paused and looked over her shoulder.

'Surely I heard something in the distance?' she exclaimed. 'Wasn't that the sound of a horse?' She shaded her eyes with her hand. 'Yes . . . it *is* a horse. It is dear Satan and Miss Smith is riding him! How *very* nice! We can all have a cosy little chat!'

She motioned the chauffeur to drive to the side of the road.

At the mention of the witch's name, Snowdrop had begun to tremble violently. Judy leant forward and murmured in his ear. 'Courage, my dear!' she whispered. 'Courage!'

Miss Smith had been riding all through the night, hunting for Snowdrop up hill and down dale, and she was neither looking nor feeling her best. When she saw the Duchess's car in the distance, with Judy and Snowdrop standing by the side, she looked and felt even worse.

A positive cloud of green smoke poured from her nostrils. She was too tired to be able to control it any longer. But she must control it. She wheeled Satan into the shade of an oak tree.

'Listen, my darling monster,' she breathed, 'this is a crisis. We must keep our heads. You must go on pretending to be *good*.'

Satan bared his teeth and shook his head.

'But you *must*,' she insisted. An evil thought occurred to her. 'Listen!' she hissed. 'If you will pretend to be good, we shall be able to get Snowdrop back again. And when we have got him back, I will let you bite him. Yes, I will.'

Satan stood quite still.

'I will let you bite him and bite him and bite him. I will let you bite him to *death*!'

When he heard this promise, Satan nodded.

For a few moments more, the witch paused in the shadows. Then she lifted her chin, took a deep breath, fixed her lips into a smile and trotted down the road.

'Here she is!' cried the Duchess, when she saw her turning the corner. 'As beautiful as ever! And dear Satan too!'

The witch drew up beside them. It was only with the greatest effort that she could prevent herself from jumping off Satan's back and starting to thrash Snowdrop on the spot.

'And what are you doing out at this early hour?' enquired the Duchess, quite unaware of the drama that was being played in front of her. 'Exercising dear Satan?'

'No, your Grace,' replied the witch. 'I have been searching for Snowdrop. He . . . he ran away.'

'Ran away? From *you*? Surely not? He was devoted to you.'

'Yes, indeed, your Grace. That is why I am so happy to have found him again.'

'So you have found him? Where?'

The witch pointed a trembling finger at Snowdrop. 'There, your Grace.'

The Duchess frowned. 'You are joking, of course.'

'No, your Grace.'

'You mean to tell me that this poor miserable creature is your beautiful Snowdrop? That is quite ridiculous.'

'It is not at all ridiculous, your Grace. And I have been searching for him all night.'

The Duchess gave a sound very like a snort. 'You are obviously very tired, my dear,' she said. 'You are . . . how shall I say? . . . *seeing* things. This wretched animal has been starved and neglected.' She turned to her neighbour. 'Am I right, Lord Goldbags?'

'Definitely,' replied his lordship.

'And yet Miss Smith seems to think that it is Snow-drop!' She shook her head. 'You have been overdoing things, my dear. You should see a doctor. Look at this poor animal again and you will realize how foolish you are being.'

Grinding her teeth but still managing to keep a smile on her face, Miss Smith stared at Snowdrop. What should she do? If she insisted that the pony was Snowdrop she would offend the Duchess, who would probably not be-lieve her anyway. And even if the Duchess did believe her, it would only make matters worse, because then she would have to explain those bruises on his back and why he was so terribly thin.

Suddenly she had an idea. 'I believe you are right, your Grace,' she said, 'now that I look at him more closely. This is *not* Snowdrop.'

Judy heaved a sigh of relief.

'However,' continued the witch, 'may I make a sugges-tion? Dear Snowdrop often feels lonely, and I am sure that he would like to have a companion. So wouldn't it be wonderful if I could take this poor creature home with me, and look after him and fatten him up? After he'd been with me for a little while he'd be as beautiful as Snowdrop is today.'

Even as she spoke she began to guide Satan in Snow-drop's direction. But Judy was too quick for her.

'No!' she cried, springing in front of the pony's head. 'He's mine. He's all mine! I bought him!'

The witch, of course, knew that this was quite untrue. 'Where did you buy him? And how? And when?'

The Duchess came to Judy's rescue. 'Really, Miss Smith,' she said impatiently, 'I cannot understand why you ask questions. We have no reason to doubt the word of this little girl. Besides, you forget that you already have one pony, apart from dear Satan. That should be quite enough.'

This was too much for the witch. In spite of the most desperate efforts she was unable to prevent quite a strong puff of green smoke from coming out of her left nostril.

The Duchess stared at her in astonishment. 'My dear Miss Smith,' she exclaimed, 'have you been having some trouble with your nose?'

The witch gulped, and murmured that it was nothing.

'But it *is* something, my dear. There it is again!' She turned to her companion. 'Didn't you see it too, Lord Goldbags? You did? Then what would you say it was?'

Lord Goldbags took a puff at his cigar. 'I'd say it was hay fever. But I've never heard of it coming out of a person's nose before.'

'Neither have I. And green, too.' The Duchess shook a warning finger at the witch. 'You must be careful, my dear. It's as I suspected. You have been overdoing things and you have caught hay fever. A very nasty sort, too, from the look of it. Supposing it were infectious? Supposing dear Satan were to catch it?'

'Quite,' agreed Lord Goldbags, who, as we know, had put a great deal of money on Satan. 'Miss Smith should go home to bed at once.'

'At once,' echoed the Duchess.

The witch still hesitated.

'Now, my dear, no nonsense!' Again the Duchess shook a warning finger. 'You are too precious to take risks with yourself. Off you go to bed! I will call and see you this afternoon.'

The witch had to admit defeat, for the moment at any rate. Forcing herself to smile, she murmured her thanks, turned Satan's head and headed for home.

Chapter Thirteen

The next days were the happiest Snowdrop had ever known. When he lay down to sleep at night, he prayed that life might go on like this forever.

Mrs. Judy had fallen in love with him from the moment she had seen Judy leading him home through the meadow. Her heart had ached for his bruises and she was so upset by his thin, starved body that she tired herself out making tempting things for him to eat and bringing him buckets of clean, cool water which she mixed with drops from her bottles of magic remedies.

What most distressed her, in the beginning, was the way he had flinched and trembled when she tried to pat him. It was as though he had been sure that he was going to be beaten. But gradually he had come to love her, and now, when she held out a lump of sugar or rubbed him with a soothing ointment, he gazed at her with wide, trusting eyes and gave a soft little neigh of gratitude.

Meanwhile, only one thing had gone wrong to spoil this pattern of happiness. And this, as you may not be entirely surprised to learn, was Mrs. Judy's Translator.

As soon as she had persuaded Snowdrop to trust her, she had led him up to the Translator in order to make him neigh into the trumpet. Obviously, he would have much to tell them; indeed, he held the clue to the whole mystery. And though the Translator was far from perfect, and sometimes seemed to produce nothing but nonsense, there had been occasions when it had been very useful indeed.

'Look what it told us about Trotsky,' she reminded Judy, as she patted the pink satin cushion for Snowdrop to sit on.

'I suppose it did,' agreed Judy, who had never had much faith in the Translator.

'There's no supposing about it. Look what it told us about Beelzebub!'

But Snowdrop seemed not to take to the Translator. As he sat on the cushion there was a loud bang. The trumpet fell off, the handle of the clockwork motor whirred round like mad and all sorts of wheels and wires and screws shot out from the side and landed in the grass.

'Oh *no*!' cried Mrs. Judy. 'It's too bad! He's broken it!'

At these words, Snowdrop began to tremble again. He felt that he had done something wrong.

'No, my dear,' she said, hurrying over to him. 'It was my fault. I hadn't realized how much weight you've been putting on in the last few days.' She wiped a tear from her eye. 'Well, at any rate, that's something to be thankful for.'

'Indeed it is,' said Judy. 'He's growing plumper every day. You mustn't take it too badly, Granny. We'll be able to put the Translator together again.'

'You've never really believed in it,' sniffed Mrs. Judy.

'That's not fair, Granny. I do believe in it . . . up to a point.'

'It's no use believing in things "up to a point",' observed the old lady. 'You've got to believe in things completely, or not at all.'

'I'll try, Granny, indeed I will.'

'There's a good girl. Just you go on trying and you'll see that one day my Translator will come into its own.

And now let's pick up the bits and pieces. We may need it sooner than you think!'

But there was another thing that was puzzling Judy.

With every day that passed the pony was growing more and more like Snowdrop. The good food and Mrs. Judy's magic ointments were working miracles. His coat was glistening again, and his bruises had disappeared. Instead of flinching when you spoke to him, he looked you straight in the eye, and made little frisking movements, as though he wanted you to jump on his back.

We know, of course, that the pony *was* Snowdrop. But Judy did not. How could she have done? This pony that she had found lying in the ditch did not look in the least like the pony whom she had seen trotting through the village with the witch's laundry cart. True, he was white, but then there are plenty of white ponies in the world. Again he was the same size, but that didn't prove anything. Ponies don't vary much, as far as size is concerned.

All the same, she was puzzled. Wherever the pony had come from, it must have been somewhere in the district, and whoever had owned him must live quite near by. Supposing they should find out, and come along and try to take him away again? Supposing they should accuse her of stealing him? What would she be able to say? Because, if we are being really honest, she *had* stolen him.

Sitting under the tree one evening, drinking dandelion tea with Mrs. Judy, she put her fears into words.

'Granny darling, may I speak to you?'

'When have I ever stopped you? Go on.'

'It's about the pony. He's growing so terribly like Snowdrop.'

The old lady put down her cup and nodded. She had only seen Snowdrop once, but she knew what Judy meant.

'Yes,' she said, 'he is. But why should that worry you?'

'What I'm going to say may sound very silly but . . . do you think he might actually *be* Snowdrop?'

'How could he be? You saw Snowdrop the day before you found the pony, and you noticed how well he looked. He couldn't possibly have got so thin in only a few hours. Unless . . .' The old lady paused. 'Unless the witch had something to do with it. I wouldn't put anything past that woman. I wouldn't be surprised if . . .'

Before she could finish the sentence their attention was attracted by a loud buzzing from above. It was Beelzebub. 'I'm sure he's got something to tell us,' said the old lady. 'If only the Translator were working!'

Mrs. Judy was quite right. Beelzebub had a great deal to tell them, because he was the only one who really understood about the witch's invention of the Puffer pills. But how was he going to explain that to them? Even if the Translator had been working it would have been difficult enough.

And then, a daring idea came into his head. Supposing he were to fly over and actually steal some of the pills? He knew where they were kept—in an envelope on the top shelf in the witch's larder. He also knew that there were words printed on the envelope, and though he could not read them, he suspected that these words had something to do with the Puffers and how they worked. If he could only get that envelope and the pills into Mrs. Judy's hands!

But would he be able to carry it? Although his wings were strong it was a long way to Meadowstream, and he would need every ounce of his energy. Still, he'd do it somehow.

All went well on his flight to the village. The wind was behind him, and as he glided across the meadows and skimmed over the tree tops, he felt as though he were floating away on some wonderful holiday, instead of embarking on a mission which might be fraught with danger. In no time, it seemed, he was over the village street and had landed on one of the laundry chimneys.

For a while he stayed there, spying out the land. Although he could not pretend to be homesick—for the witch had never given him a proper home—he was naturally interested in seeing what had been going on since he went away. The first thing he noticed was that Snowdrop's stable had been newly painted, and through the open door he could see a smart white wagon with 'Meadowstream Laundry Ltd.' printed on it. He could not read the words, but he had a good idea what they meant. They meant that the witch had been obliged to buy the wagon in order to replace Snowdrop, and he could imagine how furious she must have been about *that*. Next, he saw Satan in the meadow. He was galloping around, kicking up his heels, looking very angry. But then, Satan was always angry about something or other, so that was nothing new.

But where was Miss Smith? This was the only thing that really mattered; he must avoid her at all costs. He had no idea what she would do if she discovered him, but he was quite sure that it would be something unpleasant.

Then he remembered that at this time of day she was usually in her office counting out the money. So without any further delay he hopped into the chimney, and began to crawl down.

When he was half-way towards the fireplace he heard a sound which made his blood run cold. It was the witch . . . snoring. He stopped quite still, wondering what to do. Then he said to himself, 'Well, if she is snoring, she must be asleep. So what is there to worry about? The only thing I must *not* do is . . . buzz. I must control myself.'

He knew that this would be difficult, because whenever Beelzebub was excited, he began to buzz. And just now, he was very excited indeed.

He took a deep breath, and went on. When he came out of the dark chimney into the light, his first instinct was to fly straight up to the shelf, seize the envelope, and be off. But if he did that, he would have to buzz.

He took a deep breath, and held it in, though his lungs felt like bursting. Then, ever so quickly, he crawled up towards the shelf. Yes, there was the envelope, just as he had remembered. It was lying on its side, and he could see that there were lots of pills in it. He seized the edge of the envelope between his small shiny legs and gripped it in his mouth. And then, for he could not hold his breath any longer, out came the most tremendous buzz.

And now, the witch woke up. If you could have seen her at that moment you would have felt quite sick. Before lying down for her afternoon nap she had taken off her wig, removed her false teeth, and torn off her false eyelashes, and all these nasty things were lying beside her, in a tumbled heap on the floor. When she struggled to her feet and stepped towards him she really looked quite disgusting. She also looked very dangerous, because her skinny arms were stretched out, and he knew that her one idea was to squash him and go on squashing him.

With a single leap, he shot over her head towards what he thought was the open window. But alas, the window was not open, and his head crashed against the glass. For a few seconds he lay there, half stunned, while the witch crept towards him, growling and snarling, with her arms outstretched. 'I will squash you,' she hissed, 'squash you . . . SQUASH YOU.'

But Beelzebub had a brave heart. He did a lightning leap, which took him up to the ceiling. Then he dived towards the open doorway. The witch's fingers grazed his wings and he only escaped by the fraction of an inch. A second later, he was free.

Beelzebub's adventures were not over yet.

After escaping from the witch he had been so shattered that he could only fly for about a hundred yards, and had been forced to flutter down into the gutter, in the High Street where he hid under a heap of leaves.

For several minutes he rested there, and he would have liked to stay for longer. But suddenly it began to rain, and the water began to flow down the gutter, sweeping away the leaves that were hiding him. So he had to struggle up and climb back on to the pavement.

Just as he was opening up his wings, preparing for the long flight home, a cart came trundling down the street. It was driven by the local butcher making his weekly rounds, and he remembered that he would be driving right out into the country, within only a mile of Mrs. Judy's tree. If he could manage to hop on to the cart, he could get a lift home. That would solve all his problems.

The cart came closer and then, as it was about to pass him, he gave a trememdous buzz, and just managed to land in the back of the cart, among a pile of bundles and parcels, containing chops and sausages and that sort of thing.

He gave a sigh of relief. Now that he was safely in the cart he had to admit to himself that he had been quite frightened. It had been all very well flying to Meadow-stream, with the wind in his favour. Flying home again was another matter, burdened as he was by that heavy envelope and with the wind against him. However, all his problems seemed to be over now. He could lie back and relax and close his eyes. Unfortunately he had not noticed that he had a companion in the back of the cart, a baby that was lying asleep among the parcels. It was the butcher's baby, wrapped up in a shawl, and though it was very ugly, with freckles and a squint, the butcher was very fond of it and took it with him wherever he went. And whenever the baby wanted a sweet—which was at almost all times of the day or night—the butcher gave it one.

A few moments after Beelzebub had closed his eyes, the baby woke up. Normally, as soon as it woke up, it was in the habit of letting out a piercing yell, so that somebody should give it a sweet. But just as it was opening its mouth it caught sight of one of the Puffer pills, which had spilled out of the envelope when Beelzebub had lain down to sleep. It was lying on top of a packet of sausages, as though it were waiting to be eaten. 'This must be my sweet,' said the baby to itself. And it stretched out a podgy hand, put the pill in its mouth, and started to suck it.

Whereupon, a number of unusual things began to happen. First of all, the baby's face began to puff out, so that it looked as though it would have exploded if you had stuck a pin into it. Then its arms and legs grew bigger and bigger, and finally its behind began to get quite enormous. In case you are feeling upset about the baby, we should explain that it was not really in pain. It was not having tummy-aches, or anything like that; it was just . . . well . . . swelling out. All the same, when you are a baby, without much experience of life, you are inclined to get worried if this sort of thing happens to you. The baby was very worried indeed. It opened its mouth and let out the most tremendous yell.

The cart ground to a halt. The butcher leapt off the driving seat and dashed to the back. When he saw what had happened to the baby he gasped and seized it in his arms. At the same time he noticed Beelzebub, who had just woken up. 'It's bitten my baby,' he cried aloud. 'It's poisoned my beautiful baby!' His hand stretched out, ready to squash, squash, squash.

But once again, Beelzebub was too quick for him. Seizing the envelope in his teeth and giving a buzz of defiance, he leapt straight in the air and away. Over the meadows and over the tree tops, winging himself to safety. When he saw the Tree looming in the distance, he was so excited that he began to buzz again . . . so loudly that the envelope almost dropped from his mouth.

But he made it. And at last he dropped down on the grass, bearing his precious burden, and fell asleep.

'Whatever has happened to B?' asked Judy. 'I haven't seen him for hours.'

'Oh . . . he'll be about somewhere,' replied Mrs. Judy. 'I shouldn't worry. He knows his way around.'

It was growing dark, and they were finishing their supper under the tree.

'Listen!' said Judy. 'I'm certain I heard something. Yes, there it is again. It's B, buzzing. But where is he?',

The old lady leaned forward. 'Just under your feet, my dear. Be careful, or you'll sit on him.' She put out her hand to stroke him on the back. Then she paused. 'Whatever has he got in his mouth?'

Judy looked at him more closely. 'I think its some sort of sweet. He seems to think you might like to eat it,' she added as he hopped on to the tablecloth and dropped the Puffer in Mrs. Judy's plate.

'Very well. If that's what he wants.' The old lady stretched out her hand to pick up the Puffer.

This was the very last thing that Beelzebub had intended. There was only one thing to be done. He must eat it himself. Not all of it—just a nibble, to make them understand what it was all about.

He buzzed across, seized the Puffer, bit off a piece of the edge and swallowed it. But alas, he had forgotten how very powerful the Puffer was, and how small he was himself. If a single Puffer could make Snowdrop swell out, you can imagine what the effect of even a little bite would be on a ladybird. He began to swell out at the most alarm-rate.

Judy gave a shrill scream. 'Heavens! He's been poisoned. He's going to burst!'

'It's that sweet,' cried Mrs. Judy. 'We must get it out of him at once!'

She seized Beelzebub in both hands. By now he was the size of a tennis ball and growing bigger every second.

'This may hurt, my dear,' said the old lady gently, 'but it's for your own good.'

Pressing her hands together she squeezed and squeezed, so hard that she was afraid she might crack his wings. Suddenly Beelzebub gave a tremendous hiccup. The Puffer shot out of his mouth and landed on the tablecloth. As soon as he was rid of it, he began to shrink back to his normal size. But he was still very frightened and Mrs. Judy could feel him trembling in her hand.

'Poor little B,' she murmured, stroking his wings. 'That was a narrow squeak. Wherever did you get that nasty thing?'

Even as she spoke, Judy noticed a piece of paper lying in the grass. It was the envelope which Beelzebub had stolen from the witch. Judy picked it up and then 'she' gave a gasp of surprise.

'Granny. Look at this! It's an envelope with a lot more of those pills in it. And there's a notice on it. Listen!'

In a trembling voice Judy read out the notice.

MISS SMITH'S PATENT PUFFERS
GUARANTEED TO MAKE ALL HUMANS
AND ALL ANIMALS
SWELL OUT
TO AT LEAST
TWICE THEIR NORMAL SIZE

She stared in horror at her grandmother. 'Did you every hear anything so shocking?'

'No. But it doesn't surprise me. What else does it say?'

Judy read on:

QUITE HARMLESS TO ALL
WITCHES, WIZARDS, BATS, TOADS
AND SNAKES

Judy shuddered and stepped towards the bonfire.

'No my dear,' cried the old lady. 'Don't burn them. Those pills are evidence. So is the envelope. One day we may need them.'

'But supposing they got into the wrong hands?'

'They won't. I'll see to that. Meanwhile, let's sit down and try to work out what all this means.'

Judy sat beside her, taking Beelzebub on to her lap.

'I wish we could tell him how grateful we are,' she murmured.

'He knows,' the old lady smiled at him. 'Don't you B?'

Beelzebub gave an affectionate buzz, while Judy gently stroked his wings.

'Well, there's one thing that all this has taught us,' said

Mrs. Judy at length. 'And I don't need to tell you what that is.'

'You mean . . . the pony *is* Snowdrop, and always *has* been Snowdrop?'

'Exactly. She was starving him all the time, and it was only because she made him swallow these Puffers that he looked so fat and well. It makes my blood boil to think what that poor creature must have suffered. However, all that's in the past. What matters is the present. And the present has suddenly become more dangerous than ever.'

'Why, Granny?'

'Put on your thinking-cap. If Snowdrop is . . . well . . . Snowdrop, we haven't any legal right to him. Miss Smith has the law on her side and she might try to take him away again.'

'Oh, Granny, no . . . never!'

'There's no need to get excited, my dear. Nobody's going to take him away. I was talking about the *law*, and as you should know by now, I've never had much respect for the law. All the same we don't want to have a lot of police-men all over the place.' Suddenly she clapped her hands. 'Of course!' she cried. 'Why didn't I think of it before?'

'Think of what, Granny?'

'The Secret Meadow!'

Judy sprang up in excitement. 'Oh, Granny, I believe that would be the answer to everything! If Miss Smith ever came for Snowdrop we could hide him there.'

'We could, and we will.'

Then the smile faded from Judy's face. 'But you know how cunning she is. Supposing she were to find the meadow? It would be too terrible.'

Mrs. Judy gave her an affectionate little pat.

'No, my dear, it would not. There is something about the Secret Meadow that you do not know.'

Judy looked very puzzled. 'Something about it? Do you mean something *in* it?'

'Yes, I suppose I do.'

Judy heaved a sigh. 'I do think that you might tell me.'

'One day, perhaps, I will. But I'd rather you found it out for yourself. But now, if you'll excuse me, I think I'll go to bed. Tomorrow we'll go to the Secret Meadow And we'll take Snowdrop with us.'

Chapter Fourteen

Although the Secret Meadow was only about a mile from the House Under the Tree, you would never have known that it was there at all, unless you had lived in those parts for ages, and unless you had a very inquisitive nature.

In fact, most of the people in the district had never even heard of it. This was because of the lie of the land and all the huge trees around it, which had been planted hundreds of years ago. It lay in a hollow, like a sort of quarry, and if you had lost your way you might have stumbled over the edge of the cliffs which blocked it in from all sides. Even when you did know your way, you still had to be careful, because the cliffs were very steep.

'Are you all right, Granny?' shouted Judy, looking over her shoulder, as they scrambled downwards. 'And Snowdrop?'

'Of course I'm all right,' retorted Mrs. Judy, clinging on to a bramble. 'I may be ancient, but I've not lost the use of my limbs. And Snowdrop is fine. He's loving it.'

Indeed he was. As soon as they had come to fetch him he had realized that there was adventure in the air, and all the way to the meadow he had pranced and frisked and made funny little neighing noises. Just before they arrived he had lain flat on his tummy so that Judy could ride on his back.

'Be careful, my dear,' Mrs. Judy had cried when she saw Judy jumping on to him. But there was no need for

Judy to be careful. She had ridden all her life, and she felt as though she and Snowdrop had been made for one another.

When the three of them scrambled down the cliff and stepped into the Secret Meadow Judy gazed around her, filled with happiness. She had forgotten how beautiful the meadow was. It was all very quiet and peaceful, as though nobody had ever been there before. The tall cliffs protected them from the outside world and the great trees seemed to be guarding them. The hedges were covered with wild roses whose scent drifted towards them on the breeze. And never in her life had she seen such enormous blackberries. They were as big as plums and they were so black and juicy that they sparkled in the sunlight.

She popped one into her mouth. It was delicious. Then she picked another and offered it to Snowdrop, who shook his head politely but firmly, for ponies are not very partial to blackberries. Then she called to her granny to come and share the feast.

'No, my dear,' replied the old lady. 'We didn't come here to pick blackberries.'

'What *did* we come here for, Granny?'

'To show Snowdrop the way, of course, so that if ever there's any danger he can run here and hide before anybody can catch him. Which reminds me, you ought to start exploring to see if you can't find a safer way down that cliff.'

Judy still hesitated. 'But, Granny, was that really the only reason why we came here? You said there was something *in* the meadow. What is it?'

'As I said before, I'd rather you found that out for yourself.'

'But how can I find out if I don't even know what it is?'

'By being a good girl.'

With which Judy had to be content.

As soon as Judy had ridden off with Snowdrop to explore the cliffs, Mrs. Judy began to behave in a very peculiar manner.

First, she delved in her bag and took out an old map which she laid on the grass. When she had studied it, she looked in her bag again and took out a compass. She laid this on the map, and made several notes on a piece of paper.

Then she stared over to a far corner of the field where there were a lot of yew trees. They were very old and tall and dark, planted in two straight rows, like an avenue.

After this she closed her eyes and sat quite still. She seemed to be trying to remember something. When she opened her eyes they were full of tears. Yet she did not look really unhappy, and as she walked across the meadow she was smiling again.

When she reached the avenue, she paused and looked straight ahead of her. She was murmuring to herself, so softly that nobody could have heard what she said. Then she did the strangest thing of all. She held out her right arm, as though linking it in the arm of an unseen companion, and walked slowly down the avenue with her head held high. When she reached the end she knelt down and closed her eyes.

And that was how Judy found her when she returned from her canter with Snowdrop.

'Whatever are you doing?' cried Judy when she saw her.

The old lady jumped up and brushed the grass from her skirt. She was not too pleased at being disturbed. 'What business is that of yours?' She did not answer Judy's question. Instead she asked if she had found another way down the cliff.

'Oh yes, Granny, the most wonderful way. It's like a

sort of tunnel and I had to lie flat on Snowdrop's back or I should have knocked my head.'

'Are you sure it's safe? If so, you must show it to me.'

'We'll go at once.' Judy beckoned to the pony. 'Come along, my dear. We're going through the tunnel again.'

But for once the pony did not obey her. He had wandered over to the spot where Mrs. Judy had been kneeling and he was pawing the ground with his hoofs.

'Whatever is he doing?' exclaimed Judy, following him. 'Why, Granny, he's found something. It's a sort of stone and it looks as though it were made of marble.'

Mrs. Judy merely nodded.

The little girl knelt down and rubbed the stone with her hands. 'Why, there's something written on it. But I can't read what it says. It's covered with moss and lots of 'the letters are rubbed out.'

Mrs. Judy nodded again.

'Do *you* know what it says, Granny? You do? Is it the entrance to a secret tunnel? Oh . . . please, please tell me! What does it mean? Why won't you tell me?'

'Because, my dear, there are some things in life that one has to find out for oneself. And this is one of them.'

She walked over to Snowdrop, to show Judy that, as far as she was concerned, the subject was closed. As they set out for home, across the meadow, she turned her head and called back to Judy. 'I'm glad to tell you that Snowdrop seemed to know what it meant, at any rate, even if he can't read.'

And now we must pay another visit to Meadowstream Castle, where the witch was a constant visitor.

With every day that passed, excitement was mounting.

All along the course great stands were being built for the crowds that were expected, and a huge marquee had been put up on the lawn for the Duchess's personal guests.

'Such promising weather,' murmured the Duchess to Miss Smith, as they strolled through the grounds together. 'So bright and sunny.' She put her hand on the witch's arm in an affectionate gesture, and then drew it sharply back again, for it was as cold as ice.

'My dear Miss Smith,' she exclaimed, 'how cold you are, and on such a hot day too! Is there anything wrong with your circulation?'

'Oh no . . . nothing at all.'

'You must look after yourself. You are so precious to us.'

'You are too kind, Duchess.'

If the Duchess had been honest she would have replied that it was not entirely a question of kindness, it was also a question of money. For she had put all her money on Satan, and if the Duke had allowed her, she would also have put on her diamond tiara. But when she had suggested it, he had been quite disagreeable, and had locked it up in the safe.

In spite of the affection with which she was regarded by everybody at the Castle, Miss Smith was not happy. Everything seemed to be coming her way, and yet she was worried. It was those horrible people under the tree who were worrying her, that ghastly old Mrs. Judy and her granddaughter. That loathsome Beelzebub. If ever there was a traitor, he was one. And most of all, Snowdrop.

These were her enemies, and though she was still quite sure that she was a great deal more powerful than they were, she had an uneasy feeling that they might be dangerous. But how? What could they actually do?

If only she had somebody to talk to!

Suddenly she thought of her friend, Miss Jones, the witch with whom she had so often worked in the old days. One evening, on the spur of the moment, she decided to ring her up.

As she lifted the receiver there was the usual explosion of blue sparks, at both ends of the line. This was what they said to one another.

Miss Smith: May I speak to Miss Jones?

Miss Jones: Please hold the line, the sparks are getting in my eyes. Yes? Who is it? Oh, darling, it's you again! What can I do for you this time?

Miss Smith: I want you to come down and stay here.

Miss Jones: And where may that be?

Miss Smith: Don't be tiresome, dear. You know quite well where I live.

Miss Jones: But *why* do you want me to come down?

Miss Smith did some rapid thinking. She knew she would have to offer Miss Jones a bribe to come down from London. After all, she was a very successful witch, in a big way of business. Very well. If she must pay a bribe, she would pay it.

She took a deep breath. 'It's a little matter of murder, my dear.'

From the other end of the line, came a sparkling laugh. 'Murder, did you say, darling? Why didn't you tell me that before? If it's a nice *murder*, I should be delighted. Whom did you want me to murder?'

'Well, as a matter of fact there are two of them.'

'Splendid. But if there are two, that'll be extra.'

'And then there's a pony too.'

'That'll be another extra.'

Miss Smith ground her teeth with rage. 'I thought you made a reduction for quantities,' she hissed.

Miss Jones laughed again. 'I do. But we won't haggle

about a silly little thing like money. I'm sure that we can settle everything quite happily. Now, what would you like me to come as? What disguise? Would you like me to be a nun?'

'Wouldn't that be overdoing it?'

Miss Jones pondered for a moment. 'Perhaps it would. And in this weather a nun would be rather hot. I know! I shall come as a nurse.'

'Now that *would* be a good idea,' agreed Miss Smith. 'A nice Red Cross nurse. Nothing could be better. Have you the right costume?'

'Naturally. And a beautiful red wig to match. I've even got an ambulance to go with it. Shall I come in it?'

'No, darling. It would draw too much attention. Just the uniform will be enough. You'll bring all your poisons with you?'

'My dear, what a question! Of course I shall bring all my poisons. I wasn't born yesterday.'

'No darling,' retorted her old friend, with a hint of cattiness. 'Neither of us was.'

Miss Smith had gone to great pains to give Miss Jones a beautiful supper, and while her old friend was unpacking her suitcases she hovered round the table, putting the finishing touches to a very dainty repast.

First, she squeezed toadstool juice on to the frog spawn with which they were beginning. Next, she stirred some bluebottles into the nettle soup. After that, she poured bottled mayonnaise over a pair of iced rats which she had caught in a trap several weeks before. They smelt quite awful and she knew how much Miss Jones would love them.

As a finishing touch, she took out the skull of a goat from the linen cupboard, stuck a candle in one of its eyes, and lit it.

When Miss Jones came down she was quite enchanted.

'Frog spawn,' she cried, clasping her hands in delight. 'And nettle soup, with bluebottles! My dear, you are spoiling me! And . . . oh no . . . I can't believe it . . . these beautiful rats! They must be weeks old.' She leant over them and sniffed. 'Delicious!' She went over to Miss Smith and gave her a kiss. It was like two icicles clinking together.

Whereupon they sat down to dinner.

While they were enjoying these delicious things, Miss Smith did most of the talking. She had a lot to explain. There was all the business about Trotsky and the ostrich feathers. And Satan, and how she had tamed him. And Beelzebub, and how he had stolen the Puffers. And . . . of course . . . the Duchess. When she got to the Duchess part, Miss Jones began to get annoyed.

'Yes darling,' Miss Jones sniffed, 'I'm sure it's nice for you to meet a Duchess, but you needn't go on about it.'

'Have *you* ever met a Duchess?' demanded Miss Smith.

'Yes, dear,' crooned Miss Jones. 'Don't you remember? I gave her mumps in the London Clinic.'

'So you did,' admitted Miss Smith. 'But she recovered.'

'That was not *my* fault,' retorted Miss Jones. 'Anyway, as far as I can gather, you've not given *your* Duchess anything at all.'

'I've given her Satan,' protested Miss Smith. 'And that means a lot of money.'

'*Now* you're talking,' agreed Miss Jones, crunching her false teeth over the bones of one of the iced rats. 'Money! That's what we're here for!'

'And murder,' Miss Smith reminded her, dipping her finger into the remains of the frog spawn.

'Then don't let's waste any more time talking. Let's make a proper plan, and stick to it.'

Miss Jones had a brain as keen as a knife, and if she had not been a witch she would have made an excellent schoolmistress. She would have been very good in front of a blackboard, writing down questions, and rapping children over the knuckles if they did not know the right answers. So it was on this occasion. She went straight to the heart of the situation.

'The key to this whole problem,' Miss Jones began, 'is Snowdrop. Apart from the fact that you hate him, and want him out of this world—and I couldn't be happier to oblige in that little matter—there is one other reason why he is so important. And that is . . . *where Snowdrop goes, the others will follow*. These horrible people have obviously fallen in love with him. So what do we do? We capture Snowdrop. What happens then can be decided later. First we must get him in our clutches. After that, everything will be simple. Now, how do we get hold of Snowdrop? There are two ways. We could go along quite openly with a policeman and claim him. After all he belongs to you. That wretched girl was lying when she says she bought him at a fair.'

'I refuse to get mixed up with the police,' protested Miss Smith.

'Quite right, my dear, We've both been respectable for all these years, so don't let's start spoiling the record. That leaves only one other way. We must kidnap him.'

'How?'

A wicked smile twisted Miss Jones's lips. 'Aha!' she chortled. 'You'd never guess. Will you excuse me while I go upstairs for a moment. There's somebody up there that I'd like you to meet. I'll bring him down.'

Before Miss Smith could ask what she meant her friend had tripped away. There was the sound of a heavy suit-case being dragged across the floor, and then a series of bumps as Miss Jones dragged it down the staircase. With an effort she lifted it on to the table and paused for breath.

'What is it?' demanded Miss Smith, bursting with curiosity.

'You'll see. But perhaps it would be as well if you stepped back a little. Just for safety's sake.'

Slowly she slid back the top of the suitcase. Then, with a wave of the hand, and another wicked smile, she cried, 'Meet Otto the Octopus!'

When Miss Smith saw what was inside, she gave a gasp of delight. It was the most evil-looking octopus that you could possibly imagine. Its long, powerful arms were moving slowly around on a bed of seaweed quivering hungrily, as though seeking to strangle a victim. Its vicious mouth was wide open and its red eyes glared at her with a look of indescribable hatred.

'What an angel!' exclaimed Miss Smith. 'Never have I seen such a beautiful, adorable creature!' She stretched out her hand to stroke him.

Her friend drew her back. 'Not just yet, darling,' she warned. 'Otto doesn't trust strangers. Give him time. When he gets to know you he'll come to love you just as much as he loves me.' She gave him an affectionate pat and his whole body quivered with pleasure.

'And now, Otto darling,' she continued, 'I'm going to put you to bed again to get your beauty sleep and in the morning mummy will come along with a lovely little rabbit for your breakfast.'

She blew him a kiss and gently closed the lid.

'Well', she said, 'what do you think of little Otto?'

'I think he's utterly divine. I could hug him.'

'I wouldn't try, dear. He's quite good at hugging, himself.'

'I'm sure he is. But how can he help to kidnap Snow-drop?'

'I'll tell you. Do you remember when we were girls together and when we used to play those wild west games?'

'Of course. We used to gallop about lassoing people. Are you suggesting that I should lasso Snowdrop?'

'It's not as simple as that, dear. I'm suggesting that *Otto* should lasso Snowdrop. With your assistance. And before you start telling me that's impossible, please let me finish.'

'When you saw me bringing him downstairs, you probably thought he was very heavy. That wasn't Otto. That was the suitcase, which had to be made of lead. And all the sea water in it, which he needs for breathing. Otto's not heavy; he's all muscle. You can even wear him round your neck. In fact, I often do, and it was when I was wearing him round my neck one day that I thought of using him as a lasso. We were walking under a tree, and he was feeling playful, so I just held one of his legs and tossed him up into the branches, where there were a lot of pigeons half asleep. He came down with seven of them, which he strangled and ate one by one.'

Miss Smiths eye's gleamed with unholy pleasure. 'The sweet clever boy!' she cried. 'I'm beginning to see it all! I put Otto on the end of a lasso. Is that the idea?'

'That's it. And once he trusts you, and once you get the knack, it's as simple as falling off a log.'

'And then I gallop off with Satan and find Snowdrop and then . . . but what about the suitcase? I couldn't ask Satan to carry a heavy thing like that.'

'You wouldn't have to. He's quite happy in a plastic bag for an hour or two which you can wear round your neck. I've got one upstairs for you. It's quite a pretty one with mauve ribbons. And in case anybody wonders what's in it I've had 'Olde English Lavender' printed on the outside.'

'Darling, you think of everything,' exclaimed Miss Smith, clasping her friend's hand. Again, as their fingers met, it was like the clinking of icicles.

It would take too long to explain all the other horrible plans that the two witches worked out, as they sat up through the night. If you had listened to them you would have been extremely depressed, for Miss Jones seemed, indeed, as her friend had suggested, to have 'thought of everything'. Even if the plot to kidnap Snowdrop failed, she had other cards up her sleeve—cruel, cunning cards that she would not hesitate to play.

It was a very happy Miss Smith who went to sleep— with one eye open—that night. And a very happy Miss Jones, too.

But the happiest of all was Otto the Octopus. He realized that he had come among friends. And as he turned around on his bed of seaweed, his red eyes glowed, his evil mouth opened and closed and his thin powerful arms wound themselves together, as though he were slowly throttling Snowdrop to death.

Chapter Fifteen

$\mathcal{M}$eanwhile, back at the Tree, nobody was aware that any of these things had been happening. If they had known that the witch had a new and powerful ally in the shape of Miss Jones, or suspected the existence of such a horrible creature as Otto the Octopus, they might not have felt so easy in their minds.

As it was, life was passing by very pleasantly in the golden summer weather, with the race drawing nearer every day.

One of the reasons why Mrs. Judy found it easy to forget the outside world was because she had at last got her Translator working again, and she was eager to make more experiments with it.

'Go and fetch Dumbelle,' she said to Judy one afternoon. 'She's so small that she can't possibly damage the machine. Besides, she's always squeaking, so we ought to be able to get something out of her.'

Dumbelle had now become quite a friend of the family, and when Judy went to fetch her she made no attempt to run away, but followed her straight to the Translator.

'Now, my dear,' said the old lady, 'sit on the cushion and squeak.'

Dumbelle hestitated for a moment, and then came out with a very faint Sque . . . ee . . . ak.

'Very good,' observed Mrs. Judy. 'But try to make it a little louder.'

But Dumbelle had begun to feel embarrassed and her second squeak was even fainter than the first.

Mrs. Judy shook her head with annoyance. 'It's too tiresome,' she said. 'Why should she be shy with *us*?'

'Perhaps she's frightened of the trumpet,' suggested Judy.

'Well, the Translator won't work without the trumpet, so that's not much help. However, she did squeak twice. Let's see if it means anything.'

She drew out a piece of paper and studied it with a frown.

'What does it say?' asked Judy.

'It simply says "Cheese".'

'And what does it say the second time?'

'It says "More Cheese".'

Judy suppressed a giggle. As you may remember, she did not think much of the Translator, and it really did seem rather ridiculous to build such a complicated machine when all it could do was to tell you that a mouse liked cheese.

Aloud she said, 'Well, that's something, at any rate. It must mean that she wants some cheese.'

'Exactly. She's probably dying for some cheese, and if it hadn't been for the Translator we might never have guessed. All the same, I wish she'd said a little more.'

She let Dumbelle jump off the cushion and then she sat down on the grass.

'Judy, my dear,' she said at length. 'I'm worried. I've got a feeling that something's wrong.'

'But everything's going splendidly,' protested the little girl. 'Snowdrop's perfectly well. Nobody's come to take him away from us, and even if they did, we can hide him in the Secret Meadow. I can't see what you're worried about. Nothing's happening at all.'

'That's precisely why I'm worried. Something *ought* to be happening. Don't tell me that the witch is going to leave us in peace forever.' She sighed heavily. 'I shall be glad when this wretched race is over.'

As she spoke, there was a soft neigh behind her. It was Snowdrop.

'Now, that's a curious thing,' exclaimed Mrs. Judy. 'Whenever he hears the word "race" he neighs. It's almost as though he understood, but it may be my imagination. *You* say it, my dear, and see what happens.'

Judy went over to the pony and spoke into his ear. 'Race,' she whispered and again, 'Race!'

And now the effect on Snowdrop was really remarkable. He gave quite a loud neigh, his tail lashed backwards and forwards, and his hooves began to frisk as though he were eager to start running.

'He *does* understand,' cried Judy. 'And look . . . he's tugging at my sleeve!'

The old lady rose quickly to her feet. 'He wants to take us somewhere.' She hurried over to him. 'Race?' she whispered. 'Is that what you want? Race?'

Snowdrop now gave such a hard pull at Judy's sleeve that she almost fell over.

'Gently, my dear, gently,' she laughed. 'We'll go where-ever you want, but I can't run as fast as you can. Nor can Granny.'

Mrs. Judy gave a snort of disapproval. 'Granny can run as fast as most women of her age,' she observed. 'And a good deal faster.'

They started off across the fields, half trotting, half walking, and sometimes stopping so that the old lady should not be left behind. Very soon they realized where Snowdrop was taking them. It was to the Secret Meadow. By the time they had reached the woods and scrambled down the cliff Mrs. Judy was out of breath, but she was too excited to care.

At least they were on level ground, sheltered from the outside world, and it was not till this moment that Snowdrop let go of Judy's sleeve. After he had done so, he stepped forward a few paces, paused and turned his head.

'He's waiting for something,' whispered Judy.

'Yes,' answered the old lady. 'And I think I know what it is.' She held up her arm, making sure that the pony was watching her. Then, she swiftly brought down her arm again, at the same time crying . . . 'Race!'

With a single leap, as soon as he heard that word, Snowdrop was away, streaking like a flash of lightning into the distance. He ran so swiftly that for a moment they lost sight of him, and then he reappeared in the far corner, streaming past the avenue that guarded the stone which Mrs. Judy had discovered a few days before. Here he was, back again and on the second time he passed them he was running so swiftly that they could scarcely see him; they could only catch sight of his shining eyes and his flying mane. When he reached the end he leapt and turned while he was still in the air and started to gallop round all the four hedges of the meadow.

'I've never seen anything like it,' breathed Mrs. Judy. 'He's as fast as any horse that ever ran. His feet are hardly touching the ground.'

'It's as though he were flying.'

'I believe he'd beat anything on four legs.'

'You mean . . .' Judy hardly dared to put her thought into words. She met her granny's eyes. 'Are you thinking what I am thinking?'

'What are you thinking?'

Judy smiled. 'I'm thinking that Snowdrop wants to enter the race against Satan. Am I right?'

'Of course you're right.'

'And that's why he brought us out to the Secret Meadow. And I believe that if he were to race against Satan, he'd win.'

'He would,' the old lady replied, 'if he were left alone.'

'Oh, Granny,' cried Judy reproachfully, 'you're still thinking of the witch!'

'She's very powerful,' sighed her grandmother.

'She's not nearly as powerful as you are.'

'Don't be foolish, my dear. I'm just a weak old woman.'

'Granny, I could slap you. You're not weak and you're not old. At least, not all *that* old.'

The old lady chuckled. 'When you pay me compliments, I always know that you want something out of me. What is it this time?'

Judy drew a deep breath. 'I want Snowdrop to enter the race against Satan. That's the first thing. And I want him to win. That's the second thing.'

'And the third?'

'I want you to let me ride him.'

Mrs. Judy's reply seemed a long time in coming. She began to shake her head, and then stopped. She began to frown, and then she stopped again. Finally, she looked up to the blue sky, as though she were seeking an answer. When she gave it, her old face was wreathed in smiles.

'Very well, my dear,' she said. 'So be it. Snowdrop will race against Satan. You will ride him. And . . .'

Before she could finish the sentence, there was a flurry of hooves and Snowdrop was upon them, with a high, shrill neigh of delight.

Judy ran up and put her arms round his neck, saying two words into his ear. 'Race, race, race!' she whispered. And then, 'Win, win, win!'

And Snowdrop understood.

You would have thought that there would have been enough excitement for one afternoon, but when they returned to the tree more thrills were awaiting them.

Beelzebub was sitting on the Translator, buzzing at the top of his voice. By his side was Dumbelle, nibbling away at a piece of cheese, gobbling it so quickly that she looked as though she were going to choke. To add to the confusion, Trotsky was strutting up and down, swishing his ostrich tail in a state of the greatest agitation.

'What is happening?' exclaimed Judy. 'Have they all gone mad?'

'On the contrary,' retorted Mrs. Judy. 'They've come to their senses.'

'Whatever do you mean?'

'Well . . . look at B! Where's he sitting?'

'On the Translator.'

'Quite. And why? Because at last he's realized that it's the only way he can tell us what he's thinking. Judging by the way he's buzzing, it must be something pretty important.'

She hurried over to the machine, adjusted the trumpet and turned the handle. After a few moments she drew out the piece of paper. When she read what was written out on it, her face fell.

'Oh, dear,' she sighed. 'It's the same old story. Just a lot of nonsense.'

As soon as they heard the word 'nonsense' the animals began to make a greater din than ever. Beelzebub buzzed even louder, Dumbelle let out a piercing squeak, and Trotsky gobble-gobble-gobbled till his neck was bright purple. To add to the confusion, Snowdrop began to neigh.

'Sssh!' cried Judy, clapping her hands. When there was silence again she turned to her granny. 'Whatever we may think, darling, they don't seem to think it's a lot of non-sense. What does it say on the paper?'

'Three words. "Puffer. Snowdrop. Race." And what, I ask you, are we supposed to make of *that*?'

Before Judy could answer, Beelzebub shot off his cushion and flew to the cupboard where Mrs. Judy had locked up the Puffers.

'I don't understand any of this,' muttered the old lady, 'but he seems to want one of those horrible things.' She unlocked the cupboard and drew one of the pills out of the packet, which Beelzebub seized and put in his mouth.

'Oh, granny, don't let him eat it!' cried Judy. 'Last time, he nearly burst.'

But Beelzebub showed no signs of eating it. Instead, he flew over to Snowdrop and buzzed in front of his nose. Whereupon Snowdrop put out his tongue. Beelzebub put the Puffer on it and flew back to the Translator. Judy was about to snatch the Puffer off Snowdrop's tongue when her granny prevented her.

'He's not swallowed it yet,' she cried. 'And he's got something else to say.'

Again she turned the handle and drew out another piece of paper.

'What is it this time?' asked the little girl anxiously.

Her granny read out this message. 'It begins with the same three words,' she said. ' "Puffer. Snowdrop. Race." Then it says, "Fat Snowdrop start. Thin Snowdrop win." '

The paper fell from her hands. She stared at Judy in bewilderment. All the animals were silent, watching them.

'Well', she said at length, 'whatever this may mean, we'll find out. But in the meantime, we all ought to think of supper.'

Lying back in her rocking chair, sipping her cup of tea,

Mrs. Judy recited the message over and over again. *Puffer. Snowdrop. Race. Fat Snowdrop Start. Thin Snowdrop Win.*

'Well,' she said, 'I don't know what you think, but it looks to me as though they all want Snowdrop to take a Puffer.'

'But how *can* they?' exclaimed Judy. 'When they know what horrid things they are?'

'That's what I thought at first. But aren't we forgetting something? When Beelzebub put it on Snowdrop's tongue, he didn't shy away. In fact, he looked as though he'd have been glad to swallow it if we'd asked him to. What really puzzles me is this bit about a fat Snowdrop starting and a thin Snowdrop winning. Have you any theory about that?'

Judy shook her head.

'Well then, let's try to find one. Let's shut our eyes and try to see it all as a sort of picture. I'll tell you what I see myself. I see a racecourse with thousands of people and a whole lot of horses, all being ridden to the starting point. I see the witch on Satan, looking very proud and haughty. I see you on Snowdrop. Then—oh dear—I'm afraid the next thing I see is rather unpleasant. I see everybody laughing and booing because you're riding such a fat pony.'

'I wouldn't mind how much they laughed and booed,' said Judy, 'if only we win. But how can we, with Snowdrop swollen out like a balloon?'

Suddenly Mrs. Judy sat up and opened her eyes. 'Wait a minute!' she cried. 'How long do the Puffers go on working after they've been swallowed?'

'I can't remember,' said Judy, 'but I'm sure it tells you on the packet.'

'Then run and get the packet at once.'

While Judy was fetching it the old lady poured herself

another cup of tea, but she seemed too excited to drink it.

'Well?' she asked, when Judy returned. 'What does it say?'

Judy read out:

'The Effect of the Puffers lasts for Nearly Four Hours. After this, the Animal returns to its Normal Size within the Space of Five Minutes.'

Mrs. Judy gave a chortle of delight. 'Oh, my dear, that's quite wonderful. It means that if only we can get the timing right, we've won! Supposing the race is at four o'clock, we give Snowdrop the Puffer at twelve. At once, he begins to swell up. One o'clock comes. Then two o'clock and then three o'clock. At five minutes to four you ride him on to the racecourse. Still swollen up. And then, in the next five minutes, he goes back to normal. He becomes our own darling Snowdrop again . . . the fastest pony in the world!'

'Oh, Granny, if only it could be true!'

'It's got to be true, my dear.' She looked at Judy with a twinkling smile.

'D'you know something, darling? I'm going to back you to win!'

Judy could hardly believe her ears.

'But, Granny, a few days ago you said . . .'

'Never mind what I said a few days ago. Things are different now. We know a lot that we didn't know before. And one thing we know is that when you ride out on Snowdrop, the odds will be a thousand to one.'

'What does "odds" mean?'

'It means that if you have a pound in your money-box, and if you put it on Snowdrop, you will make a thousand pounds.'

'Oh, Granny, you're joking!'

'I never joke about money, my dear. It's far too serious

a subject.' She smiled and nodded to herself. 'It'll feel quite peculiar to have a little money for a change.'

Judy's eyes were sparkling. 'What shall we spend it on?'

'There'll be plenty of time to think about that when we've got it.'

Chapter Sixteen

Judy went to sleep that night with a smile on her face. So did her granny. So did Snowdrop and Dumbelle and Beelzebub. The only one who did not fall asleep with a smile was Trotsky, because turkeys, unfortunately, are not very good at smiling. Their beaks don't seem to be designed for that sort of thing. But he *felt* like smiling, and as he curled himself up he made soft little gobbling noises, which showed how happy he was.

However, the smiles would have faded from their faces if only they could have overheard what Miss Jones was telling Miss Smith in the witch's parlour.

For there was one thing they did not know—a very terrible thing, too. *Miss Jones had discovered the Secret Meadow.*

Yes . . . when they had gone out with Snowdrop that morning, she had followed them. She had ridden out with Satan to the tree, disguised in her Red Cross uniform, with the idea of spying out the land. And then, just as she had turned into the field, she had seen Judy and her granny setting out with Snowdrop and she had guessed that something important was happening. And she had trotted softly after them, keeping in the shadows and hiding behind the hedges. When they had disappeared through the secret entrance, she had made her way up to the top of the cliff, and peered through the branches. And she had seen it all. She had seen Snowdrop leaping in the air, racing round the field like lightning, twisting and turning with incredible speed. What is more, Satan had seen it too, and he had been so enraged that he could hardly stop from plunging down the cliff and biting everybody in sight.

When she had learned all there was to learn, she galloped back to Meadowstream, to tell her friend Miss Smith, only to discover that Miss Smith had been summoned to see the Duchess. So she had to wait until the evening before she was able to talk things over with her.

Miss Smith arrived in the Duchess's Rolls-Royce shortly after six, looking very smart and very pleased with herself. But as soon as she heard what had happened, the green smoke poured from her nose in such profusion that the room was quite thick with it and Miss Jones began to choke.

'Darling,' she gasped, 'you must try to control yourself.'

'I can't,' sniffed her friend. 'I'm too angry.'

'But what is there to be angry about? Nothing has changed.'

Miss Smith blew her nose violently. 'Everything has changed,' she snapped. 'If that horrible pony is as fast as you say . . .'

Before she could finish the sentence Miss Jones interrupted her. 'You're not suggesting that he's as fast as Satan?'

'It was you who suggested it.'

'I did nothing of the sort. You told me that Satan was the fastest horse in the world. If he isn't, you've brought me down here under false pretences.'

She was almost as angry as her friend, and she began to pace the room, snapping her fingers so fiercely that sparks flew from them.

'It's too bad,' she continued. 'Look at all the trouble I've gone to! Look at all the expenses I've had! Look at all the money I've put on that wretched horse of yours!'

'How *dare* you call Satan a wretched horse? 'cried Miss Smith. 'He's the wickedest, fastest, most beautiful horse in the world, and if you say he isn't I shall scratch your eyes out!'

'Oh, you will, will you?' hissed Miss Jones, stepping over to the corner of the room. 'We'll see what Otto has to say about that!' As she spoke she threw open the lid of the box in which Otto was sleeping. No sooner had she done so that he woke up and began to hiss, and his cold slimy tentacles crept out over the edge of the box in Miss Smith's direction.

'No, darling!' screamed the witch. 'Please ask him to go to sleep again.'

'Only if you apologize,' snorted Miss Jones.

'I do . . . I do.'

'Then say you're sorry.'

'I'm sorry.'

'And so you should be,' snapped her friend. She bent down and gave Otto a kiss. Then she folded his arms and slid him back into the box.

'And now,' she said, 'perhaps you'll listen to *me* for a change. The first thing you do is go to bed.'

'Go to bed? At this hour?'

'Yes. I know it's only seven o'clock but you'll need all the sleep you can get before the race tomorrow.'

'And what will you be doing?'

'What I shall be doing is my own business.'

Miss Smith ground her teeth with rage. But she managed to keep a smile on her face. 'Just as you say, darling. I leave it all to you. As long as you get hold of Snowdrop.'

'I'll get hold of him,' snapped Miss Jones. 'I'll get hold of him so tightly that he'll never escape. And when I've got hold of him, the others will follow. That ghastly old woman and that hideous child and the turkey and all the rest of them.'

'And then what will happen?'

A terrible smile crept over her friend's face. 'I shall just leave them to Otto,' she murmured sweetly. 'And when he's finished with them they'll wish they'd never been born.'

Miss Smith heaved a long sigh of gratitude. 'If only I could be there to see it all!'

'Well, you won't be,' retorted Miss Jones. 'You'll be in bed. Which is where you're going at this very moment.'

Five o'clock was striking from the old church tower when Miss Jones got up from the sofa where she had been sleeping and tiptoed upstairs to let Otto out of his box. As she lifted the lid he began to hiss with pleasure, not only because he was tired of being shut up but also because he guessed that some sort of wickedness was in the air—something really bad, in which he would be able to show how clever he was. Perhaps his mistress was even going to ask him to strangle somebody. He could imagine nothing that he would enjoy so much and the thought of it made him hiss all the louder.

'Ssh!' whispered Miss Jones, as she slipped him into her plastic bag and hung him round her neck. 'Miss Smith is still asleep and we mustn't wake her yet.'

Then she crept downstairs out into the courtyard. When she opened the stable door Satan gave a neigh of excitement, because he too had guessed that something evil was afoot and he wanted to be part of it.

A few moments later they were on their way.

As they trotted down the village street, Miss Jones, in spite of her appearance of self-confidence, was feeling rather worried. She was beginning to realize that the task ahead of her might be more difficult than she had imagined.

It was all very well for Miss Smith to say 'Capture Snowdrop and the rest of them will follow,' but when she had captured them where was she supposed to take them? Besides, it might not be so easy to capture all of them. If she had only Snowdrop to think of that would be simple, because Otto would only have to throw one of his tentacles round the pony's neck and he would be dead in less than two minutes. But during those two minutes a lot of awkward things might happen. The old lady would certainly attack her and so would the little girl, then the turkey might try to bite her eyes out and she did not like the thought of that poisonous beetle. Of course, being a witch, she had plenty of spells up her sleeve, but it takes time to weave a spell. For instance, it takes nearly half an hour to bring a person out in spots. There was only one thing to be done—she would have to deal with Snowdrop first and make sure that he was safely out of the way before tackling the others. This meant that she would have to go very carefully and ride very silently, so that she would catch them unawares.

'Ssh!' she whispered to Satan, as they went along. 'Softly—softly!'

Satan understood. He kept to the soft grass by the side of the road and as they drew nearer to the House Under the Tree he slowed down and crept forward as silently as a cat.

Under the tree they were all asleep, but Snowdrop was sleeping more soundly than any of them, because he was having such beautiful dreams. He dreamt that he was scampering through the loveliest meadow in the world, where the grass was greener than he had ever seen before and the buttercups more golden, and where the white flowers of the daisies were made of the sweetest sugar which he could bend down and crunch whenever he was out of breath.

And then suddenly in his dreams a cloud came over the sun and the skies grew dark and the wind blew cold, and he began to shiver and tremble as though a shadow had fallen across him. And in the distance he heard a hiss, a long-drawn out 'His . . . ss . . . sss' that drew closer and closer and louder and louder . . . till it seemed to be echoing in his very ear.

In a second he was wide awake, and when he saw who was standing above him his blood ran cold.

For he was staring straight into the cruel blood-shot eyes of Otto the Octopus. And slowly, slowly creeping towards him was a long, slimy arm that curved and quivered like a snake. It came closer and closer and then it paused, only a few inches from his throat.

And then he heard the echo of the witch's laughter. 'That's right, my sweet,' she cackled. 'Take your time about it. He can't escape us now!'

Snowdrop tried to stagger to his feet, but his legs seemed to be frozen. The witch laughed even louder and as she laughed she patted Otto's cold grey head. 'Yes, my darling,' she murmured, 'you're going to enjoy this, aren't you? And so am I. So don't hurry it. Tickle his throat for a moment, just to show what's coming to him!'

As soon as she had spoken, she realized that she had made a fatal mistake. For she had forgotten that Otto's arms were icy cold, and that when they touched a person or an animal they gave out a powerful electric shock.

And that was just what happened. The instant that Otto's arm came in contact with Snowdrop's throat the shock was so sharp that he jumped to his feet and was away. He jumped so high and turned so swiftly that before

Miss Jones knew what was happening he was half-way across the orchard.

'Follow him!' she hissed, digging her heels into Satan's flanks. 'Don't let him escape!'

Satan bared his teeth and leapt forward in pursuit. A few seconds later they were plunging into the under-growth that guarded the Secret Meadow. Satan ran so fast that Miss Jones had to cling tight to his mane to stop herself falling off. The brambles were cutting into her face and Otto was curling his arms round her neck, but she did not care. She was filled with such a fierce hatred of Snow-drop that she would have gone through any torture to destroy him.

Now they were plunging down the cliff and out into the meadow, with Snowdrop only a few yards ahead of them. 'Faster, faster!' she yelled.

They were almost within reach of him. The witch grip-ped one of Otto's tentacles making ready to throw him on to the pony's back. Only a few more seconds to go.

'Now!' snarled the witch.

She hurled the octopus forward.

And now comes the strangest part of our story.

For as soon as Otto's arm touched Snowdrop, the octopus gave an agonized hiss and slid to the ground. And when he had fallen he began to twist and turn and hiss all the louder.

'What is happening?' cried the witch. 'Go after him! Throttle him!' At the same time she urged Satan forward.

But Satan stood still and began to tremble.

'What is the matter with you all?' she screamed leaping from Satan's back.

And then she too began to tremble. For she had seen what Snowdrop was standing on.

It was an old slab of stone, covered with moss. A

churchyard stone. Yes—many years ago, before any of us were born, there had been a church in this corner of the Secret Meadow. It was in this very church that Mrs. Judy had been married when she was a girl of eighteen. Though it had long since disappeared and though the world had passed it by, it was still a sacred place which the powers of evil could never conquer. If witches or wizards or any of their evil companions ever try to enter a church, they drop dead as soon as their feet touch the threshold. And that is what happened to Otto. He had fallen straight on to the stone which had marked the place of the ancient altar and it had destroyed him as swiftly as if he had been struck by lightning.

Chapter Seventeen

If some kind person had provided you with a helicopter during the next few hours, so that you had been able to fly over the scene of these adventures, you would have come across so many exciting things that you would hardly have been able to keep pace with them.

The first thing you would have noticed would have been huge crowds of people all making their way to the racecourse. They came in cars and in buses and on bicycles and on foot—so many of them that there were traffic blocks for miles around. Standing at one of the windows of the Castle, the Duchess watched their arrival with great satisfaction, because they all had to pay two shillings to get through the gates.

'It is too wonderful,' she exclaimed to the Duke. 'Apart from the money we shall win on dear Satan, we shall make thousands of pounds out of the tickets. I shall be able to buy a new tiara.'

'You already have three,' the Duke reminded her. 'That should be quite sufficient.'

'In these days,' she observed, 'one can never have too many tiaras.'

And then, if you could have flown over the fields to Meadowstream, to see what was going on at the laundry, you could have watched something even more exciting . . . the return of Miss Jones with Satan, and the frightening scene which occurred when she met Miss Smith.

Let us imagine that we can step out of the helicopter and listen to the two witches as they faced each other in the courtyard.

'What have you been doing to Satan?' cried the witch. 'He's shaking all over. He looks as though he'd seen a ghost.'

'We have both seen a ghost,' retorted Miss Jones. 'Or something very like one.'

Her friend snorted with impatience. 'Don't talk nonsense. And where, may I ask, is Otto?'

Miss Jones's only reply to this question was a stifled sob.

'What's wrong with you? Why don't you answer me? What have you done with Otto?'

'Otto,' sniffed Miss Jones, 'is dead.' As she spoke, tears came to her eyes. If you had never seen a witch weeping, you would have been quite alarmed, because witches' tears are always freezing cold and roll down their cheeks so that they form icicles under their chins.

'Dead?' Miss Smith's voice rose to a scream. 'Dead? Does that mean he hasn't killed Snowdrop?'

Miss Jones sniffed even more loudly and wiped the cluster of icicles from the end of her chin. 'My darling Otto is dead,' she repeated.

By now the witch could scarcely speak. 'Stop nattering about Otto,' she gasped. 'What do I care about that smelly old octopus? *What has happened to Snowdrop?*'

For a moment Miss Jones stood there in silence. She could scarcely believe her ears. And then, as she slowly realized the meaning of the witch's words, she was filled with so fierce a fury that she turned away in order to conceal her feelings. Otto—her darling Otto—had been called 'a smelly old octopus.' This was something she could never forgive. Otto—her faithful friend, the best and wickedest octopus that the world had ever known—had been grossly insulted. Oh . . . Miss Smith would pay for this! She clenched her fists and ground her teeth, thinking out a plan of revenge.

Yes she would pay for it, and dearly! But before she could think out a plan of revenge she must try to control herself. After a few moments she managed to do so. The icicles on her chin melted as swiftly as they had come and when she turned round she even managed to smile.

'Don't let's quarrel, darling,' she murmured. 'There is nothing to worry about. Snowdrop is dead.'

The witch stared at her suspiciously. 'Are you sure?'

'Quite sure. And it was Otto who killed him. Otto died for your sake. For both our sakes.'

The witch heaved a sigh of relief. 'Oh, Miss Jones!' she cried. 'How can I ever thank you?'

'There is no need to thank *me*,' sighed her friend. 'It is Otto whom we must thank.'

'Of course. Darling Otto. How bravely he died! And how lovely to be friends again.'

The witch blew her a kiss. 'And now,' she said, 'I must give Satan his breakfast. He will need all his strength before the day is over.'

She led Satan off to his stable, shutting the door behind her. When she had gone, the smile faded from Miss Jones's face her expression was terrible to behold. 'Revenge . . . revenge!' she muttered to herself. But what sort of revenge? Should she poison Miss Smith, or give her something that brought her out in boils? That would be quite easy, boils were Miss Jones's speciality. For that matter, she could bring Satan out in boils, too. The only trouble was, that if she brought him out in boils, he would not win the race, and she would not make any money from him.

But did she really *want* Satan to win the race? She was not so sure. Supposing Snowdrop won it? From the way he had run this morning it seemed quite possible that he might be as fast as Satan—even faster. The more she thought of it, the more excited she became. If Satan were to lose the race, Miss Smith would be ruined. Utterly ruined. She would not only lose all her money, she would lose all her friends; indeed, she would make a great many enemies and her reputation in the world of witches would be gone forever. She would be made a laughing-stock. Miss Jones would see to *that*. She would telephone to every witch she had ever met and tell them the whole story and by the time she had finished Miss Smith would never dare look people in the face again. And even if she did, her own face would be so covered with boils that she would probably prefer to remain in as dim a light as possible.

But the boils must wait. Before she began to mix her boiling powders she must work out a plan to make sure that Satan lost. She sat there, thinking furiously, and if you could have seen her face you would have turned away in horror.

Even so, for a moment you might have felt sorry for her, because in spite of her rage she was still weeping. The tears were still trickling down her cheeks and the icicles were still forming under her chin. You see, she really had been very fond of Otto, and now he was dead.

But he would be revenged!

And now, let us slip back into our helicopter and fly over to the tree, and see what is happening to Snowdrop.

Supposing that we land quietly in the orchard, and tip-toe through the trees, what shall we find?

What we find is rather surprising. For there, sleeping happily in the long grass, is Snowdrop, looking as though he had not a care in the world.

How could this have come about? Well, that is difficult to explain. This is a story about magic and magic is hard to put into words. All we can tell you is that after those few terrible moments when he had felt Otto's cold slimy arms slithering round his neck, after he had shaken himself free and seen the octopus twisting and writhing on the stone slab, he had suddenly felt a great strength, as though some hidden power had come to his aid. He was no longer frightened; he was quite certain that he would be able to meet whatever trials there might be ahead. He could not have explained this. After all, he was only a little pony with a very simple mind. But just as there are times when animals can scent a danger which is hidden from ourselves, so there are times when they know that the danger is past. This was one of those times, which was why, when Satan and Miss Jones had galloped away from him leaving a trail of angry sparks behind them, Snowdrop was able to trot quietly home and lie down to sleep in the orchard and go on sleeping till the sun was high in the heavens.

'I really think we ought to wake him up,' said Judy.

Mrs. Judy glanced at her watch. 'Yes, the time has come. Even if it hadn't, we can't keep the others quiet much longer.'

This was true. All the creatures around them were in a state of such excitement that they could scarcely control themselves. Dumbelle was darting about in the long grass uttering shrill squeaks and Beelzebub was buzzing about like a crazy bumble-bee. The most agitated of them all was Trotsky, who was longing to gobble-gobble at the top of his voice and could not understand why Judy kept saying 'Sssh'. All he wanted was to tell everybody how happy he was and it was most frustrating to be 'sssh'd', because it meant that instead of doing a proper 'gobble-gobble' the only noise he could make was a sort of subdued hiccup, which sounded like 'glug-hoch-gob-gob'.

'Yes,' repeated Mrs. Judy. 'The time has come.'

'And ought we to give Snowdrop the Puffer now?'

Again the old lady consulted her watch. 'Let me think,' she said. 'It's twenty minutes to twelve. The race is at four o'clock. The Puffer takes exactly four hours before it works off again. So he must have it in twenty minutes' time.'

Judy sighed. 'Does he *have* to have it? I'm afraid it might give him a pain.'

Her granny nodded. 'I've wondered about that, too. But I'm sure it doesn't give him a pain. At the worst, it only makes him feel rather uncomfortable, as though he'd eaten too much for dinner. Anyway, it's for the last time. He'll never have to take one again.'

'And you really think it's important?'

'I'm quite sure it's important. If Snowdrop's going to win, we've got to take everybody by surprise. Particularly Satan and the witch. They must never guess what's happening—not till the very last moment when it's too late for them to do anything about it.' She gave Judy an affectionate little peck on the cheek. 'And now, my dear, supposing you go and put on your things and let me see how nice you look in them.'

Judy ran off to change. During the last few days Mrs. Judy had been busy making her a jockey's outfit, and as she slipped into the white breeches and pulled the pink silk shirt over her head she thought what fun it would be to have been born a boy.

'Splendid!' cried Mrs. Judy, when she showed herself again. 'But the cap's not tight enough. We mustn't let you show any of your pretty curls. Let me put a stitch in it. And while I'm doing that, you can go and see to Snowdrop.'

And now, time seemed to fly on wings. Snowdrop swallowed his puffer as though it were a piece of sugar, and as soon as it began to work he stood up and shook himself, and gave a loud neigh, as though he understood everything that was happening. Meanwhile Dumbelle and Trotsky and Beelzebub gathered round him, squeaking and gobbling and buzzing to their heart's content. They were so thrilled that when the time came for them to leave Mrs. Judy had difficulty in persuading them to get into the old hat-box in which she was taking them to the race.

At last they were ready.

'Let me look at you all,' said Mrs. Judy, wheeling out her bicycle. 'Snowdrop first. Yes, my dear . . . perfect! Your own mother wouldn't recognize you. And now, Judy. Wait a minute, darling! There's still a curl showing under your cap. That's better. Nobody would know you weren't a boy. And now Dumbelle and Beelzebub . . . that's right. And Trotsky . . . get into the box . . . and stop gobbling and keep your head down.'

She gave a final pat to Snowdrop and a last kiss to Judy.

'Well, my dears,' she cried, 'what are we waiting for?' A moment later she had jumped on to the bicycle and was pedalling away towards the open road.

And that is how they set off to the Great Race. If you had seen them on the way, you would certainly have turned your heads in surprise and thought what a funny collection of creatures they were. For what *could* have been funnier? An old lady on a bicycle, with a cardboard box strapped to the back and a turkey's head pushing through it, and a lot of buzzings and squeaks coming out of it. And behind her, a little girl dressed like a jockey, in a pink silk shirt, riding a pony so fat that it could scarcely keep up with them. As they drew nearer to the racecourse the crowds became thicker and they laughed louder. Little boys thronged round them and pulled Snowdrop's tail and little girls chased the bicycle and pulled Trotsky's feathers. But the old lady cycled straight ahead and Judy kept her seat and went on smiling. They might laugh now, but when the race began it would be a different story.

All the same she was thankful when they had passed safely through the gates and when, with a final wave to her granny, she trotted off to join the other horses to take her part in the Grand Parade.

Three o'clock. A quarter past three. Half past. A quarter to four. A little while ago time had seemed to be flying, but now it seemed to crawl.

Judy stayed well in the background, keeping her eyes on her watch. Two things were worrying her. Firstly, where were Satan and the witch? Why had they not yet appeared? However, even as she asked herself the question, it was answered by a great roar from the crowd as Miss Smith galloped towards them. As she drew nearer Judy had to admit that she made a most impressive sight. Her jockey's shirt was covered with sequins that sparkled like diamonds in the sunlight and there was a golden feather in her cap. As for Satan, he looked blacker and swifter than ever, with his teeth bared in a hideous grin. They passed so near to Judy that she could have put out her hand and touched them, but they showed no sign of recognition except for a scornful laugh from the witch as she noticed how ridiculous they looked.

But her second problem was more urgent; would the Puffer work off in time? There were only fifteen minutes to go, and surely by now Snowdrop should have begun to shrink? Had they made some dreadful mistake? The very thought of such a thing made her tremble and she leaned forward to whisper in the pony's ear.

'Please, darling Snowdrop . . . please try to make the Puffer work. Please try to hurry it up . . . for my sake,' As she spoke she stroked his soft white neck and though Snowdrop did not speak her language he understood her meaning, and he knew that the time had come for him to make a great effort. So he began to breathe very quickly . . . in and out, in and out . . . as though he were trying to get rid of an evil spirit. And as he breathed, quicker and quicker, Judy realized that he was indeed shrinking. But was he shrinking fast enough? He was still far too fat and already horses were lining up for the Grand Parade.

And now the Parade began, with Miss Smith riding Satan, haughtily tossing her head to show off the golden feather in her cap. Then came the other horses showing off their paces and finally Judy, a long way behind. As they started trotting slowly round the course she had the impression of a sea of faces, all staring at her, and all mocking her and she could hear a storm of laughter as she rode by. But gradually the laughter began to die down and as she turned to face the crowds she saw that the people were no longer laughing; they were staring in astonishment. For Snowdrop was shrinking faster and faster; he was no longer a figure of fun; instead of a great puffed-up creature he was becoming slim and swift and beautiful. The whole great crowd began to whisper together. 'Something's happening,' they muttered to one another, 'something we don't understand.'

Three minutes to go. The Parade was over and the

horses were lined up at the starting point. It was at this moment that Satan turned his head and noticed Snowdrop standing by his side. The effect was immediate, as though he had been given a powerful electric shock. He leapt into the air so suddenly that the witch's false teeth were almost jerked out of her mouth. Then he let out the most terrible howl of rage. But it was nothing as to the scream that came from the witch. She had believed Snowdrop to be dead. And here he was, standing next to her. What's more, the boy who was riding him was smiling—but no, it wasn't a boy, it was that awful girl . . . it was Judy.

Judy went on smiling. It was a brave smile, because she could feel the hatred that was sweeping over her; she was trying not to be frightened. It wasn't easy. Satan looked so huge and so wicked and so swift. And she felt so small and so weak. She leant forward and stroked Snowdrop's neck with trembling fingers. It felt warm and somehow comforting. She smiled again, sat up in her saddle, and looked straight ahead.

'They're off!'

For the first few seconds Judy scarcely knew what was happening. She was deafened by the roar of the crowd and half blinded by the glare of the sun shining straight in her eyes. Apart from that, Snowdrop had leapt forward so swiftly that he had almost thrown her off her saddle. But she righted herself, pulled her cap over her eyes and realized with a thrill of delight that she was out in front leading the whole field with nobody ahead of her.

But her joy was short-lived. Behind her she heard a thud of hooves and out of the corner of her eye she saw the powerful body of Satan, drawing alongside. Nor was that all she saw, for hot red sparks were coming from his mouth and behind the witch there was a trail of bright green smoke.

'Faster . . . faster!' she cried to Snowdrop, but her words were drowned in a fiendish cackle of laughter from the witch, like the scream of a bat, and she could feel Snowdrop shuddering beneath her, as though the sound had struck him to the heart.

And now they were ahead of her. Only by a few feet, but that was more than enough. It was only a short race and she could already see the winning post in the distance.

Then it happened. Satan stumbled. The huge black body lurched and staggered, as though he had tripped over a stone, and the witch slithered forward over her saddle with a strangled scream. Again Judy drew alongside, and again she was ahead. But once more the thud of hooves overtook her, once more Satan was in front.

And then, he stumbled again. This time he was lost. For the witch lost her grip, and was unseated, and crashed on to the turf in a cloud of smoke.

The tears were streaming down Judy's cheeks as she raced past the winning post. Snowdrop was so exhausted that when she jumped off him he sank on to the grass as though he would never rise again. Judy knelt by him, whispering words of comfort . . . but the cheering from the crowd was so fierce that she doubted whether he would hear them.

But one sound they both heard. A very simple sound— just a buzz. Right in her ear, buzz-buzz-buzz. And as she looked up, she saw where it came from. It came from Beelzebub, who had alighted on her shoulder, and was blinking at her with his small red eyes.

Suddenly she understood. It was Beelzebub who had won the race. He had flown out of his basket and whirled above them, and when he had seen what was happening he had shot forward at the vital moment and stung Satan on the nose. And when that was not enough, he had shot forward again and stung him very hard indeed on the behind. It may not have been a very lady-like thing to do, but I think we shall all agree that Satan deserved it.

Our tale is nearly over. The time has come to say good-bye and the best place to say it, surely, would be under the tree, where they were all sitting down to supper with the moonlight shining down upon them.

It was the most wonderful supper that anybody could ever have had. In the centre of the table sparkled the golden cup which Judy had carried away from the race-course and in the cup were a thousand golden sovereigns. It had been handed to her by the Duchess, who had made a most gracious speech . . . with some effort, because she was not feeling all that gracious after Satan's defeat. However, although she had lost a lot of money on Satan, she had made much more from the sale of the tickets, so— as she observed to the Duke—she would be able to buy another tiara after all, even though it might not be quite so large as she had hoped.

Around the golden cup, arranged all over the table-cloth, were plates loaded with the most delicious things to eat. There was a huge plate of cheese for Dumbelle— Cheddar cheese and Dutch cheese and French cheese—all cut into convenient slices. There was an equally huge plate of corn for Trotsky, which Mrs. Judy had made even more appetizing by mixing it with nuts and raisins, so that when he ate it he felt as though it were Christmas-time. There was a wonderful salad for Beelzebub, made out of the petals of buttercups and the leaves of baby lettuces. And for Snowdrop there was the hugest bowl of all, piled high with sugar that glistened in the moonlight like a little silver mountain.

'And now, my dear,' said Mrs. Judy, 'I think we should both drink a toast.'

She rose to her feet and lifted her glass.

'To Snowdrop', she said.

'To Snowdrop,' echoed Judy. She took a sip and gave a gurgle of laughter. 'Granny darling, I believe this is your dandelion wine.'

'It certainly is,' replied her granny. 'Which is why you mustn't have too much of it, because it's very strong.'

Judy looked around her. 'Couldn't the others have some too?'

'Certainly not.'

'Not even a tiny sip?'

The old lady smiled. 'Very well. Just for once. As it's a special occasion.'

So Judy took her glass and dipped her finger in the wine and went round the table. First she gave a little to Snowdrop, who promptly sneezed. Then to Dumbelle, who squeaked more shrilly than she had ever squeaked before, because it tickled her throat, Then to Trotsky, who took rather too much, so that he began to hiccup; and then he tried to gobble his thanks he got very mixed up. Like this: '*Gobble hic gobble cup pickle kickle gibble gobble kick gob giggle cup.*' Just try to say that aloud and you will see how strange he sounded.

Finally she came to Beelzebub. He was so tired that he was already half asleep, but he managed to open his eyes. Judy dipped a blade of grass in the dandelion wine and very gently touched him with it, so that it rested on the tip of his nose like a dew-drop. 'Buzz-buzz-buzz' . . . whispered Beelzebub. And then even softer . . . 'buzz . . . buzz.'

　　　　　And at last . . .

And so we can leave them, in the light of the summer moon, with peace in their hearts. And we can close with the words that bring all good stories to an end . . . 'And They Lived Happily Ever After'.

But there is still one last question to be asked for this—as we were almost forgetting—is a story about a witch.

What happened to Miss Smith?

We will tell you.

After Satan had stumbled and sent her sprawling on the grass, she was so shocked that for a few moments she lay there quite still, listening to the other horses thudding past her. All her hopes and dreams had crashed around her, and for the first time in her life she was afraid. Although she was still a very powerful witch, she had been playing the part of a human being, and at this moment she was surrounded by thousands of real human beings who had every reason to hate her. And to hate Satan too. She had let them down . . . and now they would be after her blood . . . she must escape.

She scrambled to her feet and if you had watched her during the next few minutes you might almost have been tempted to admire her. The first thing she did was to tear off her golden wig. Then she threw away her long false eyelashes, and finally she tore out her false teeth and wiped the lipstick from her mouth. Then she crawled onto Satan's back and rode him slowly towards the crowds which were surging towards her. And though they recognized Satan, they let him pass when they saw that he was being ridden by this old hag who—so they imagined—could not possibly have anything to do with the golden-haired young woman whom they were seeking.

So the witch escaped, and when she was safely out of sight she rode full tilt across the open country in the direction of her favourite haunt, the little wood with the evil-smelling pond where she had been used to collecting the frog-spawn. Her plan was to hide there till darkness had fallen, and then to ride quietly into the village when everybody was asleep. After which she could steal into the laundry by the back entrance, take away all her money and anything else she could lay her hands on and simply disappear into the night. She would leave behind her a trail of debts and no doubt the police would be searching for her, but that did not trouble her in the least. They would never catch her.

So she reached the wood and stayed there by the pond, where Satan refreshed himself by taking great gulps of the disgusting water, which was full of slime and tadpoles. From time to time she scooped up a handful of frog-spawn, which tasted even more delicious than usual. The hours passed by, night came down and when it was completely dark she went on her way.

The village drew nearer and then, suddenly, she called Satan to a halt, staring in front of her. What was that light in the distance? And what was that bitter odour in the air? Where did they come from? Urging Satan forward again she reached the side streets and dismounted. Creeping round a corner, she saw in an instant what had happened. The laundry was on fire! It was blazing so fiercely that even if the fire brigade had been able to get through the flames and the smoke they would never have been able to save it. She had lost everything. She was totally ruined.

Or was she?

For as she stood there, fuming with rage, she heard a faint sound in the distance—the sound of a warning bell—clang, clang, clang—nearer and nearer—louder and louder. And now, round the corner, swept an ambulance and it was being driven by Miss Jones.

So that was what had happened! It was Miss Jones who had started the fire, and it was Miss Jones who was running off with all her money! But she wouldn't get away with it. She would strangle her first, poison her, cut her head off—she would get Satan to trample on her and bite her up into little pieces.

Leaping on his back she set off in pursuit and in a few moments had overtaken her. Then she wheeled round and stayed in the middle of the road, barring the way.

The ambulance came to a halt with a scream of brakes. Miss Jones, staring ahead, felt suddenly afraid, as well she might. Satan was straddled in front of her, with sparks streaming from his nose. Miss Smith was crouched in the saddle as though she were about to hurl herself through the windscreen.

'Darling,' murmured Miss Jones, in a trembling voice, 'thank goodness I've found you.'

'Where is my money?' hissed the witch.

'In the boot, of course. I was on my way to give it to you.'

Miss Smith made no comment on this monstrous lie. She stayed there panting and glaring. She was so enraged that she had a good mind to tell Satan to charge forward at that very moment, and smash the windscreen with his hoofs, and start biting her to death without delay.

But gradually she calmed down. She had had a tiring day, and though she was quite certain that she had Miss Jones at her mercy, it might be better to wait a little while till she had thought of some particularly horrible way of disposing of her.

'In the boot, you say?' she repeated. 'Open it!'

Miss Jones jumped down and hurried to the back of the

car. When she opened up the boot Miss Smith saw that it was packed with all her bags of gold. There was also all her laundry and the Duchess's laundry too, all her wigs and a crate loaded with tinned frog-spawn and bottled rats.

'You seem to have thought of everything,' she observed shortly.

'Yes, dear, I did indeed. I was nearly burned to death rescuing all your little treasures.'

The witch nodded. It occurred to her that burning Miss Jones to death might be a very agreeable way of spending next Sunday afternoon.

Aloud, she said, 'Well, my dear, I'm sure I'm very grateful.'

Miss Jones sighed with relief. The danger seemed to have passed, at any rate for the time being.

'And now,' she said, 'you must get in beside me and we will drive away.'

For a moment the witch did not reply. She was rummaging in the boot for one of her wigs. She pulled out a beautiful red one and stuck it on, and when she had added a fresh pair of eyelashes and popped in a new set of false teeth she was quite her old self again.

'*Too* becoming,' exclaimed Miss Jones, secretly thinking what a frightful old hag she looked. 'But now we really must be on our way. And dear Satan can trot along behind us.'

And so they set off through the night, choosing the loneliest roads and the narrowest lanes. If you had met them you would have felt a chill of fear, for as they drove along a cloud of bats flew out of the trees to join them and circled round the car, squeaking and screaming and fluttering.

Miss Jones waved to them and blew them a kiss.

'Sweet, wicked little things,' she whispered. 'It's nice to think that we still have *some* friends.'

Miss Smith nodded. She was beginning to feel less enraged with her companion. Perhaps she would not burn her to death after all. Just scorch her for an hour or two in front of a nice slow fire.

'What are you thinking of, my dear?' enquired Miss Jones, gently stroking a very large bat that had perched on her wig.

'I was wondering which of us was the wickedest witch in the world.'

Miss Jones gave a tinkling laugh. 'Oh, my dear, what a question! Why . . . *you*, of course.'

Miss Smith shook her head. 'You don't really mean it. You're only saying it to be nice.'

'But I *do* mean it, darling,' She gave her a sidelong glance and once again she thought that she had never seen such a ghastly old horror. The new wig only seemed to make her look worse. 'After all,' she murmured sweetly, 'you've been at it for at least a hundred years longer than little me.'

Miss Smith made no reply. But if you had been watching her closely you would have seen a very faint wisp of green smoke coming out of one of her nostrils. And that, as we have already learned, was a sign that she was not amused.

These are other Knight Books

Margaret J. Baker

THE MAGIC SEA-SHELL

Michael, Merry and Betsey Toppling's father is missing in the Antarctic. Their mother runs a seaside boarding-house to provide for them all. It is in the boarding-house that they find the magic sea-shell – at the back of a drawer that has not been opened for years. Through the sea-shell they meet a mermaid who can grant their wishes by magic and in doing so leads them into unusual adventures.

Christianna Brand

NURSE MATILDA

Mr and Mrs Brown were always having great difficulty with their numerous and incredibly naughty children. They tried all the agencies but nurses, governesses and nannies never stayed long with the Brown children 'The person *you* want is Nurse Matilda,' they were told. And when Nurse Matilda does arrive, strange things begin to happen.

NURSE MATILDA GOES TO TOWN

Once Nurse Matilda made Mr and Mrs Brown's huge family of incredibly naughty children all good and well-behaved, but now they are naughty again. The children go to stay with Great-Aunt Adelaide in London – and once more Nurse Matilda has to be called to the rescue.

These are other Knight Books

Elizabeth Goudge

THE LITTLE WHITE HORSE

The little white horse belonged to the Moon Princess, who lived centuries before Maria Merryweather heard her sad story. But Maria, now living in the mysterious old Manorhouse of Moonacre, finds herself closely involved with what happened to the Moon Princess so long ago.

SMOKY-HOUSE

The Smoky-House inn at Faraway is the home of the Treguddicks and their very intelligent dogs Spot and Sausage. Mathilda, the bad-tempered donkey, completes the family. Even in the days of smuggling, when most of the neighbourhood is afraid of the Man-with-the-Red-Handkerchief, Faraway seems happy and contented. But danger comes suddenly very close and it takes the children and the animals, with the help of the Good People, to save everyone.

Otfried Preussler

THE ROBBER HOTZENPLOTZ

The wicked robber Hotzenplotz was the terror of the village. Whatever he wanted he stole and he was always armed with a sword, a pistol and seven knives. Then he took Grandmother's musical coffee mill and Kasperl and Seppel just had to do something about it. But the ingenious plan misfired and robber Hotzenplotz captured them both. When Kasperl was sold to the great magician Petrosilius Zackleman there seemed no way of disentangling themselves from such a fix.

THE FURTHER ADVENTURES OF THE ROBBER HOTZENPLOTZ

The robber Hotzenplotz escaped from prison, still as wicked as ever. And something just had to be done about it, so off went Kasperl and Seppel to trap him. Then everything went sadly wrong and he kidnapped Grandmother and captured them both too. All seemed lost until a crocodile-dog called Fido arrived on the scene and justice triumphed once again.

"BB"

THE FOREST OF BOLAND LIGHT RAILWAY

The Forest of Boland Light Railway, with its magnificent steam engine the Boland Belle, is the pride and joy of the gnomes who live in the forest. But one day their enemies the leprechauns overcome the gnomes in a surprise attack, and drag them off to their stronghold, Castle Shera. The outlook seems bleak, but the cowzies come to the rescue just in time.

THE WIZARD OF BOLAND

The gnomes of the Forest of Boland are horrified to find a dragon sleeping in a cave near their village; but the wicked Wizard Homm is delighted to see the dame dragon browsing among the willows in the forest because he needs some dragon's blood to work his best spells. But the Wizard's greed is his downfall . . .

Mary Stewart

THE LITTLE BROOMSTICK

Nothing could ever happen here, thought Mary, exiled to Great-Aunt Charlotte's house. But she was wrong. That very day Tib the cat led her to a curious flower called fly-by-night. Then she found a little broomstick hidden in a corner – and her strange and wonderful magic adventure had begun.

This book belongs to

Lucy gillmore

THE WICKEDEST WITCH
IN THE WORLD

Miss Smith has some evil plans to get up to plenty of tricks and make a fortune.

But Miss Smith is a well-established and truly wicked witch of four hundred years' standing. She and her allies Beelzebub the beetle, Otto the octopus, and Satan the horse are opposed by Judy, Mrs Judy and the beautiful pony Snowdrop. The real trial of strength comes in the Race at Meadowstream.